Distant Worlds

S.F. Lydon

Copyright

No portion of this book may be reproduced or distributed in any form without permission from the Publisher

Names, characters, products, etc. are used from the author's imagination, as this is a work of fiction. If there is any resemblance to any establishment or person living or dead, it is purely coincidental

COPYRIGHT© 2022 Ibis Publishing LLC

Contents

The Book of Sha 5

The Covenant 19

To Forge a Soul 37

A New Purpose 52

The Waypoint 67

A Sea of Sand 90

Awakening 102

The Cost of Vengeance 126

The Ten Towers of Tarah 149

The Coming Storm 166

The Book of Sha

Perdos was hopelessly lost. The forest around him was a tangle of thick foliage and clinging undergrowth. His boots were soaked through from days of rain, and his clothes were threadbare at best. His hair, so blond it was almost white, was plastered to his head. His hazel eyes were dull and red-rimmed from lack of sleep. The long scar along his jaw, running fom his ear to the side of his chin, ached in the cold air.

Since escaping from his master several weeks ago, Perdos had fled westward. He did not know how far it was to the end of the Empire's lands, but he knew that west was his only hope. He had walked until he could barely stand every day. Hiding for short times wherever he could find a likely spot. He knew pursuit must be behind him; the Thyric Throne was notorious for being harsh with escaped slaves.

Little was known among the slaves of the Thyric Emire what lay beyond the borders to the west, other than the Throne had never been able to push that boundary. In all the world of Olthos, only this western part of Thyria and the lands of the Alephi to the far north had remained free. The Empire had conquered all else; Pellum and Noros to the east, ancient Matar to the south, and the wild islands known as the Kels had all fallen to the might of the Throne.

Perdos' stomach rumbled, not for the first time today. Hunger had become one of his constant companions. He had scavenged fruits, nuts, and even the occasional beetle or worm. But his stomach had not been full since his escape. His feet ached unceasingly, his eyes burned from lack of proper rest, and fear tinged everything he saw or heard. These were his only friends now; hunger, pain, exhaustion, and fear. They were also the only thing that kept him sane, or near to it. These constant pulls on his mind were all that kept him believing he was still alive and not caught in some endless fever dream.

Thirst was the only acquaintance that had not come calling for days now. With the near constant rain, he was always able to find some pool or source of runoff to assuage his thirst.

A stray branch caught his side and scraped along his skin through his thin shirt. It stung, but he barely noticed such things anymore. He could not count the number of scrapes and bruises he recently accumulated. He wanted so badly to stop and collapse in a pile of leaves and close his eyes. He did not even particularly care if they opened again.

The sound of hounds in the distance brought Perdos out of his brief reverie. The braying cut through the night air like a harsh word in a silent room. He had first heard the hounds three days before. In an effort to cover his scent, he had bathed in a shallow pool and then smeared his body with as much mud as he could manage. He believed that was the only reason he had not yet been found.

Without another thought, Perdos ran until he reached the first climbable tree he could see. It was a young elm, and it had several strong boughs low enough for him to use to haul himself up off the ground. He scrambled upward through the tree until the limbs got too thin, and he could go no further. He was at least thirty feet up that point.

Perdos could hear the hounds more clearly now, though he wasunsure if that was because he was so much higher up or if they had truly gotten closer. Caution dictated that he assume the latter. The braying of the beasts was north of him, somewhere within several miles, he guessed. Though in truth, he was no fair judge of such things. He knew very little woodcraft and knew nothing about hounds other than that their teeth were sharp and their legs were faster than his own.

Perdos stayed in the tree for quite some time, and he would have been thankful for the rest if it had not required such concentration to remain in his perch. He had gone too high to sit comfortably on the branch that held him, and he dared not try to sleep for fear he would be found unawares.

It was not the first time that Perdos wished he had a weapon. He had no idea how to fight with one, but he was reasonably fit for a man who had spent his life doing slave labor and, more recently, fleeing that life with little sustenance. He resolved to find a branch that could serve as a club when he got down from the tree.

If he got down from the tree.

Perdos added that thought almost unconsciously now. The 'ifs' in his life had piled up rapidly in the last few weeks. Nearly every thought now required the caveat of 'if' to accompany it. 'If' he found food, 'if' he found shelter, 'if' he could sleep for a bit. So many 'ifs'.

The only 'if' he did not consider or did not allow himself to consider, was the 'if' he managed to find some other, more hospitable land. If he managed to make good his escape for real… but no, it did not bear thinking about yet.

The braying of the hounds was beginning to grow faint. They seemed to be turning further north. Perhaps they thought he might be heading for the mountains to seek shelter among the Alephi. It was a thought that had occurred to Perdos at times, but all the stories he had heard about the bearded, barbarian Northmen agreed that they were unwelcoming to strangers.

Finally, Perdos felt safe enough to risk leaving his perch. He took his time descending the tree; it would be just his luck to fall and break his neck just when he felt a measure of safety. He reached the ground in one piece and set about searching for a branch he could use as a club if he needed it. He found one that would serve; it was about three feet long and as thick as his bicep with a large knot at the end.

Perdos resumed his trudging through the woods. Even though the hounds had left the area, other forms of pursuit could be nearby. He could not let himself stop yet.

It was nearing dawn when Perdos heard the sound of moving water. He followed it and found a river too thick to cross, but at least he would have drinking water if the weather dried out. The undergrowth was too thick near the river, and the ground was too muddy for him to follow its course directly. Plus, he would be better hidden in the trees.

Perdos continued his trek, keeping the river on his right, using the sounds of rushing water to follow its course from far enough back that he could not see the river itself. Two days passed like this. He rested occasionally but never for more than an hour or two. An hour or so after his latest rest, he heard a great rushing and crashing of water. It was a sound he had never heard before, and moved cautiously towards it.

Perdos reached the end of the trees, exposing a clearing on the edge of a cliff. The river poured over the cliff in a furious rush not a hundred yards to his right. He walked to the cliff's edge and was stunned by what he saw.

The land fell away immediately; the cliff face was as sheer as could be. Perdos could not begin to guess at how far the fall was, but it must have been at least a thousand yards. The water struck the base of the cliff at the eastern end of a great lake. The river continued on its way at the western end of the lake. His eyes followed the water, but as he watched the river wend its way westward, he realized what he was seeing.

The land was utterly uninhabited. Or at least, no sizeable population must be there. It was all lush forest and green hills for as far as Perdos could see. Which, given how high up he was, must have been for miles and miles.

"Hello," a voice said behind Perdos. He spun, so startled he almost stumbled backward over the cliff's edge. He raised his makeshift cudgel in a fashion he hoped made him look like a competent warrior.

A man sat on a log at the southern edge of the clearing. He sat beside a small fire.

Perdos was shocked that he could have walked past the man without seeing him. He was an older man with dark eyes, iron-grey hair, and a beard to match. He was of average height and a slim build, but there was a strength to him. He bore no weapon that Perdos could see but a walking stick made of an unfamiliar wood was propped up beside him.

"W-who are you?" Perdos asked, his stick still held before himself.

"I've been waiting for you," the man said. He remained sitting, ignoring Perdos' question, and prodded at the fire with a small stick. His eyes were locked on Perdos. There was something in him that frightened the escaped slave.

"What do you mean?" Perdos asked, a hint of desperation in his voice. The old man did not appear to be Thyric; in fact, he had an accent that Perdos had never heard before. "What do you want with me?"

"I mean what I said," the stranger said, simply. "I have been sitting here, waiting for you." He eyed Perdos as if a bit perturbed. "You certainly took your time getting here."

Perdos could do nothing but stare back wordlessly at the man. Surely, this was some mistake.

"By damnable rowan, it took you nearly a month," the old man went on. "Talet isn't so far as that." There was a tone of exasperation now.

Perdos was unsure what was damnable about rowan; it was just a type of wood. And how could this man know what city he had been enslaved in? This was all so far beyond him. Maybe he had finally gone mad.

"Oh, come now," the stranger said, the exasperation growing. "Come sit, and I will explain myself. To start with, I am no slave-taker. I swear by burning salt and bitter iron, that I will not bring you back to your life of slavery."

Perdos was again mystified by the strange man's words. Burning salt? Bitter iron? Such unusual things to swear by. But there was something in the man's voice, a sincereness that Perdos could almost feel. He did not know if believed the man, but he *wanted* to. He slowly approached the fire, and seated himself on the ground across from the stranger. He kept his cudgel in his hands.

"I think we can do without that," the man said, eyeing the branch. "I did not sit here for over a month just to kill you. And even if I did have such intention," his eyes took on a different sort of intensity, "you could not stop me with just that stick. Or at all, really."

"What is your name?" Perdos asked again. "And how did you know I'd be here? And what do you want with me?" The questions poured out of him; unsettled by the man's less-than-veiled threat, he needed answers.

"Well now," the man said, "let's take it one at a time. To start with, you may call me Isar." He looked to one side, a thoughtful expression on his face. "Yes, I think I like that. Isar," he said, seemingly to himself. "Anyhow, as to who I am, well, I am a servant of sorts. I serve a master greater than any other. I serve the One True God. His name is Sha, and he sent me to save your kind from the yoke of the Thyric Empire."

Perdos was nonplussed. One God? Everyone knew there were many gods. The

Thyric pantheon had hundreds. "But why have you been waiting for me?" Perdos pressed the point.

"Well," Isar said, "I am afraid I cannot do the things that Sha needs of me. Not alone. I need someone else. Someone who can lead the downtrodden, broken slaves of the Empire. I, or more accurately, they need one of their own to lead them. And Sha had chosen you."

Perdos' head was spinning. This was beyond surreal. He was definitely insane now. This could be nothing more than a dream or perhaps a nightmare. Some small part of him, a part that had longed for heroism and a greater fate, had taken control of his mind.

"I have something for you," Isar said reaching into his cloak. He pulled out an old, leatherbound book. It was worn but in decent shape. He held it out to Perdos. Perdos took it, held it in his hands, and looked back at Isar.

"I can't read," Perdos said as though it was apparent; which it should have been. He had been a slave. Of course, he could not read!

"I think you will find," Isar said, "that you can read this book." He smiled a strange smile, his eyes alight. "Give it a try."

Perdos opened the book. He studied the lines of the first page, lines that were utterly incomprehensible to him. But, the more he looked, a strange sense of understanding came over him. He could not read it exactly. But he understood what the page said, or at least he believed he did.

Perdos looked up at Isar, who was grinning like a cat that had cornered a three-legged mouse. Perdos did not like that look, but he was still astounded by this odd phenomenon.

"How is this possible?"

"Anything is possible through Sha," Isar said with the gravity of a pious man. Still, Perdos had reservations. Another thought struck suddenly in Perdos' mind. Isar had said he had been waiting for over a month. But it had been less than a month since Perdos had escaped.

"How did you know I would escape? And how did you know I would come here?"

"Anything is possible through Sha," Isar repeated, though this time it was with less solemn piety and more of the teasing tone of someone who has another at an extreme disadvantage. Perdos supposed that was precisely the case.

"To get down to the meat of it," Isar said, serious now, "if you come with me, learn from me, and maybe, just maybe, trust me, I can turn you into the leader that Sha needs." He eyed Perdos with intensity. "I can teach you to use the knowledge in that book. I can teach you to call upon Sha's aid and to wield power that any other mortal could only dream of."

Perdos considered this. It was still insane. But something in Isar's voice was almost hypnotic. Perhaps he was lying. Or perhaps, he was simply wrong. Or, just maybe, he was telling the truth. Beyond all those 'maybe's and 'perhaps', there was the simple fact that Perdos had nowhere else to go. He had no other options.

And, Perdos could not deny the idea of becoming the savior of his fellow slaves. A hero come back among them with his new God to save them from their lives of misery. That thought, most of all, was a burr in his brain. It stuck to him and needled at him.

He could be a hero.

Perdos looked Isar in those dark, intense eyes of his; his mind made up.

"Teach me."

The Covenant

Weyris sat among the trees of the Penitent's Grove, striving to remain calm. His long white hair hung down past his shoulders; his long thin beard lay upon his thin chest; a chest that rose and fell with each deep breath of the sweet Fae air. He watched the sun hanging high in the sky, knowing that when it reached the horizon, his fate would be determined.

Weyris never thought to be in this position. To be bound in the Penitent's Grove, the place meant for those awaiting judgment for the worst of crimes, was not a position he ever would have thought to find himself. The polished stone bench beneath him was cold and hard. The *ranna* trees that surrounded him were tall and silent; patient sentinels that held him captive more tightly than any armed guard could. That was the power of the Grove. Once set inside its bounds, a prisoner could not leave them unaided.

For nearly two days, Weyris had been waiting here. He knew why it was taking so long. First, the Council had to be convened. Then, they would need to deliberate on whether the accusations against him had merit, which they certainly did. In this case, they would also need to discuss the matter of Weyris' fellow prisoner. He was not sure where Almenisar was being held, but it was likely somewhere terrible. For Almenisar, they had likely gone to lengths they had never had before. The strongest containment spells, bonds carved of *ranna* wood and set with runes of suppression, and of course, cold, bitter iron.

Weyris considered also his crimes. He was guilty of them, that was certain. But perhaps their circumstances might be enough to grant him a pardon. Or at least, not the terrible punishment he feared. But even if that sentence were handed down, he would bear it. He had done what needed to be done.

The sun was almost down now. Soon they would be coming for him.

And no sooner did Weyris have that thought, footsteps sounded beyond the edges of the Grove. Three figures entered the Grove. They were tall and thin, like most of their kind. Narrow faces with large, canted eyes of brilliant hues framed by long, fine hair. Long, pointed ears showed through their hair, like the noses of some shy forest creature, poking out to scent the evening air. Weyris knew all three of them, though this was not such a strange thing in the Fael. The Faen was not so numerous that many of them remained unknown to their kin. Kestrel, Harlowen, and Felara were their names. Kestrel and Harlowen had been friends of his once, back before his sin. Felara though, well, she had always disliked him.

Harlowen carried a wooden object in his hands as they approached him. Weyris knew what it was without being told; he held out his arms, wrists together before Harlowen even reached him. If Harlowen was surprised by Weyris' simple acquiescence, he did not show it ;instead, he simply unfurled the wooden manacles and snapped them around Weyris' wrists. He beckoned wordlessly for Weyris to rise and follow, which Weyris did with no attempt at conversation. He knew that they were forbidden to speak to him under these conditions.

As they walked from the Grove, Weyris studied the manacles. They were carved from *ranna* wood. They were as hard as iron and most compatible with the Arts of the Faen. He could see the minuscule runes carved deeply, but intricately in the wood. They were hard to read, but he knew what they were meant to do. They were runes of binding and blocking; they would stop him from using any form of Expulsion or Absorption so long as he wore them.

Weyris and his escort stepped out of the trees and onto the path leading toward Atantris. As always, Weyris was struck by the beauty of the greatest city of the Faen. Glass towers stood throughout the city. Glass structures of every hue, and many that changed hues as the light shining through them changed angle, pierced the sky all across the skyline. Some towers stood ramrod straight, and others twisted at what the mortals would have called impossible angles. He would never get used to the majesty of the sight. It was even more captivating now that it might be his last look at it.

They entered the city and walked through the streets. There was no plan to the city's layout, but it did not appear disordered. Each building seemed to be placed exactly where it belonged. They were not simply in the city; they were *of* the city. They belonged, to put it simply, as a tree belongs in the forest.

The buildings were as varied as could be. Some were made of stone; river rock, greystone, and even obsidian. Others were made of wood; ash, elm, or oak, but not rowan. No, never rowan.

The streets they walked were so finely paved that the cobbles seemed to be carved from the ground rather than set side by each and mortared into place. Trees and other plants grew all over. Some in gardens, others by the side of the road. Their presence was neither planned nor accidental; like everything else, they simply were there and felt right.

As the sun was beginning to vanish behind the horizon, they arrived at their destination. It was a great bowl carved down into the bedrock of the city. Benched lined each level of the depression, falling in tiers to the smooth stone floor at the bottom. A stage lined one end of the flattened bottom of the bowl. Two stone pedestals stood at the other end, each facing the stage. The stage had twelve seats made of comfortable yew wood, and they were already occupied.

The Forum was ready for the trial and the Council of the Fair Folk, the Great Lords of the

Faen, were prepared to sit in judgment. Weyris knew this was coming, but he still had difficulty fighting the nerves that turned his stomach. His escort led him to the floor and over to one of the stone pedestals. They fastened his manacles to the ring of stone that rose from the top of the pedestal, which came up to Weyris' waist. They left him there, alone and vulnerable to the eyes of all who would soon be gathered to observe the proceedings.

Weyris observed the Council; he knew most of them by sight. Yelhan and Yelhara, the eldest of the Faen and the only twins ever born among them, occupied the two middle chairs. If the Faen Council could be said to have leaders, it was those two. Their faces were impassive beneath their snowy locks.

To their right sat Renaris. He was young to be on the Council, but was accounted very wise and fair. After him, there were Hemloral and Paverra, two well-respected Faen women. The other two beside them, Weyris did not know.

On the left of the twins sat Lauriet. She was a severe woman, well known for her loathing of mortals. Beyond her were three whom Weyris also did not know. In the last seat was a woman of remarkable beauty, even for a Fae. Her midnight hair fell to her waist. Her eyes were pools of dark blue, like the sky before full dark. He was surprised that she was here, for Dendenna rarely deigned to leave the Twilit Twilight Grove, even for a matter such as this.

The sound of feet on the stone floor drew Weyris' attention away from the stage. To his right, three unfamiliar Fae led a disheveled figure in loose grey robes. The newcomer's long grey hair hid his face, but Weyris knew who it was.

Almenisar had arrived.

Almenisar's escort attached his wooden manacles to the other stone pedestal, just as Weyris' had been. When Almenisar raised his head, Weyris saw the collar of bitter iron that had been locked around his neck. It was disconcerting to see any Fae so bound, but Weyris had been prepared for this. Almenisar had made his own bed.

Other Faen began to fill the seats of the Forum. Soon, the entire place seemed packed to the point where many had to stand at the lip of the bowl looking down. Weyris could feel their eyes on him. He could feel the weight of their curiosity and condemnation like a stone yoke over his shoulders. It was unpleasant, to say the least.

Finally, Yelhan and Yelhara stood. The rest of the Council remained seated, and the sounds of the onlookers faded quickly.

"The Forum is in session," Yelhan began. "Let no one interrupt these proceedings under penalty of expulsion from the Forum for the duration of the session."

"We are here," Yelhara continued, "to determine the true events of these past years in the mortal lands and to determine the guilt of these two, Weyris of the Yew-Slope House and Almenisar of the Sleeping Stone, who are known to have been heavily involved in these affairs."

"Do either of you deny your involvement in the events in question?" Yelhan spoke again. When neither Weyris nor Almenisar spoke up, he continued. "Very well. We shall proceed."

"To shed some background on these events, we invite Loremaster Shi'ewe to speak." With that, both Yelhan and Yelhara resumed their seats. The Loremaster rose from the first level of benches and took the floor before the stage.

"Almost a decade ago, as the mortals count it," Shi'ewe began, "a large group of slaves rebelled against the Thyric Throne and escaped from their bondage. They traveled west and came upon the lands that were, until recently, our last refuge in the world of Olthos." The Loremaster took a breath and looked around. "We welcomed them, and for a time, we shared that place, which the mortals named the Free Lands. But soon after, the Thyric Throne sent an army to reclaim their errant property. With our aid, the mortals threw back this army and several more after. The mortals called this the War of the Freeing. At the same time, a new religion sprang up among the mortals. They called their god Sha, and at first, we believed it nothing more than mortal fancy."

Weyris could see the events in his head as they were described. He had been there after all. He remembered the wars. The horror of the battles. The smell of blood and death. He fought down a shiver as the memories came on and on.

"When the last battle of those long wars came," Shi'ewe went on, "the battle the mortals call the Battle of the Bloody Hills, we learned how wrong we had been. This new religion was a thing of power. Old power. The followers of this 'Sha' called up horrors we had never seen before. They devastated the land, and after that battle, we last remaining Faen in the mortal lands decided to withdraw here, to the Fael, for good." He shook his head, his long beard wagging over his stomach. "A few of us made a study of this religion and the things that they had wrought. And I can say, without a doubt, that the creatures they summoned were surely the denizens of Neth Gellin, and the lord they worship is none other than Asha'tamenar'ash himself. Worse yet, we discovered how this travesty came to be. For it was none other than one of the accused, Almenisar, who gave them the knowledge to breach the veil and commune with the Great Leech!" His anger stoked to a white, hot flame. And he was not alone. Shouts of outrage and horror rained down from the rising tiers of the Forum.

Yelhan stood and raised a hand, murmuring to himself. Suddenly, a great gust of wind rushed through the Forum. It drowned out the voices of the crowd and brought silence back.

"Thank you, Loremaster," Yelhan said. "Almenisar, do you deny these charges?" Again, the grey-haired Fae remained silent. Yelhan nodded. "Then we will consider them proved, and a fitting punishment will be decided upon."

Lauriet stood up suddenly, making a motion to Yelhan. He seemed to hesitate before yielding the stage to her. Lauriet looked at Almenisar with a gaze full of fury.

"Do you have nothing to say for yourself, traitor?" Her voice was full of venom, although she did not shout. Her words roused something in Almenisar, however. He looked up at her, his eyes almost empty.

"It had to be done," Almenisar said softly, almost too softly to hear. "I did what I had to do to prove that the fences of Neth Gellin can be breached. They are not secure." His voice began to pick up in strength. "We need to take measures against Asha'tamenar'ash. Not someday, not soon, but now. He will be free again and when he is, we will need the Nine to stand against him. I have spoken of my theories. I urge you all to listen one last time."

"Bah!" Lauriet sneered. "We have heard of your theories, Almenisar. But you have never offered anything beyond that. You have no proof that your plan will work as you say. And we will not help you to destroy the ten worlds that our masters created on some wild whim of yours."

"It is not a mere whim—" Almenisar was cut off by Yelhara standing abruptly.

"We are not here to debate your theories," Yelhara said. "We are here to determine guilt and assign punishment. You have condemned yourself with your silence, and now doubly so with your words. Your guilt is assured." She motioned to Lauriet and again toward her brother. Lauriet sat bitterly and Yelhan stood again.

"There is another matter to settle here," Yelhan turned his eyes on Weyris. "Weyris of Yew-Slope, do you deny passing the secrets of the Waypoints to a mortal known as Oryll the Mariner?"

"I do not deny it," Weyris said. "I too did what I had to do. I needed to know if Almenisar had given the same knowledge to other people on other worlds. So, I asked Oryll, who is known to many of us if not personally, then at least by name and deeds, to visit the other worlds and find out whether the cult of 'Sha' had been spread there."

"Your reasoning is immaterial," Yelhan said. "You broke one of the oldest of our laws, and you will be punished for it." Weyris had known from the beginning that this would be the result. But he had still felt it necessary to voice his reasons.

Yelhan spoke to each Council member on his side of the stage, while Yelhara did the same to those on the left. They came back together in the middle and conferred briefly.

"The Council was much in deliberation over the past days," Yelhan said, "deciding on what the punishments should be, should you both be proven guilty."

"Your guilt has been proven," Yelhara continued, "and so the agreed upon rulings must be handed down." Weyris had dreaded this moment, but he steeled himself; he would not go to the Rowan Tree like a coward.

"It has been decided," Yelhan pronounced, the weight of judgment in his voice, "that you Almenisar of the Sleeping Stone, and you Weyris of Yew-Slope, shall be banished from the Fael for the rest of time. You shall leave by the Waypoint this night, and you may never return."

Weyris was shocked. Banishment? Such a thing was unheard of. In all the years of the Faen, they had put people to death or imprisoned them. But banishment! That had never been done.

The sound of laughter broke the stunned silence that had filled the Forum. Weyris was shocked to see it was Almenisar who was laughing.

"Banishment?" he said, with something close to derision in his voice. "Fine! Banish me! But I will continue my work! I will bring the Nine back! And when Asha'tamenar'ash is free again, you will all cry my pardon for not believing in me!"

"No," Weyris said it before he realized he was speaking. "No, Almenisar, you will not succeed in your mad plan, for I will be out there too. And I will oppose you in all things. I swear it; by root and bough, stream and stone, ash and elm. I will thwart you in all your mad designs."

Almenisar stared at Weyris with some mix of shock and loathing. The Forum around them was deathly silent. It seemed for a moment that they were the only two beings in a distant galaxy, standing on opposite sides of a *lunis* game board. The sounds of arguing on the stage brought Weyris's attention back to the Council. They were arguing over this new development. He could not hear the details, but it seemed to be growing out of hand.

"I believe," a musical voice lifted above the others, "I have a solution." It was Dendenna. The Mistress of the Twilit Grove was standing now, facing the other members of the Council. "Or as close to a solution as we might find." The others stared at her, some incredulous, others entranced by her soothing voice. "I suggest a Covenant."

The others looked thoughtful, particularly Yelhan and Yelhara. Almenisar looked angry.

"I will never consent to a Covenant with him!" he shouted. He would have gone on, but Dendenna fixed him with a almost pitying smile.

"We do not need your consent," she said with a touch of condescension. "Not with the twelve of us here." It was true, Weyris considered. Twelve Lords of the Faen would be powerful enough to bind them against their will. Even if it was a frowned upon practice. Almenisar paled a bit at her words.

"Shall we have a vote?" Dendenna asked. She lifted her hand in an almost lazy air. Weyris could not tell if she was genuinely unconcerned by the gravity of these proceedings or simply incapable of appearing concerned. One by one, the other members of the Council raised their hands.

"Well then," Dendenna said with a touch of satisfaction. "Let it be done."

"Very well," Yelhan said. "The Council has decided that a Covenant shall be created between Weyris and Almenisar, that—" Yelhan paused as Weyris raised his hand. "Yes, Weyris?"

"If I am to walk among the mortals, my lord," Weyris said, "then I shall take a mortal name. I ask that you call me Waylan." All the Council, the surrounding Faen that he could see, even Almenisar, were staring at Weyris as if he had gone mad. Perhaps he had.

"As you say," Yelhan said after a moment of consideration. "Let a Covenant be formed between Waylan and Almenisar. That they may neither harm nor actively thwart each other in any way. And that neither may return to the Fael, while the Ninestars hang in the night sky."

Each Council member raised their hands, closed their eyes, and began to chant. They called upon the Nine, the sky, the sea, and the earth to bind Waylan and Almenisar. They called upon all the elements of the world to seal their binding and to follow them both with it wherever they went. The chanting lasted a long time, but when it was done, Waylan could feel something settle over him. Like an invisible rope, slack now, but at any moment, it might pull taut.

"It is done," Yelhan announced. "You are both now banished from the Fael and bound by the Covenant. May the Nine watch over and judge you justly from here on out."

To Forge a Soul

It was late at night in the town of Tarm. The sky was clear and the moon was full. The stars were bright; the Ninestars, brightest among them, hanging in their familiar arc. At the edge of town sat the smithy. It was the only building not dark, despite the late hour. The fire from the forge shone with a warm light, bathing the smith in its red-orange glow.

The smith's name was Andon. He was a tall man with shoulders like an ox and arms thicker than the thighs of most men. He had short brown hair and stormy grey eyes. He was also widely regarded as one of, if not the, best smith in all of Bendel; maybe on all of Trallis. He stood staring at the mostly finished blade lying on his worktable. It was a typical sword in most senses; bright steel nearly three feet long. The only oddity about it was the triangular hole set in the broadest part of the blade, near where the hilt would start.

It was a complicated shape to forge. Or at least, to forge well. The blade had to be strong enough to hold together and function as a proper sword, even with the empty space. It was a difficult mold to make and even more challenging to make a steel strong enough to suit it. Andon was one of the few smiths with the talent to make such a thing.

It was this exact skill that drew his customers. Andon's work was too great for anyone in Tarm to afford, as he had been told many times by wealthy would-be patrons offering to whisk him away to one of the larger cities and set him up with a shop there. They talked of how rich he would become working for the gentry. They spoke of all the wonderful things he might make for people who could afford more than horseshoes and cheap nails. He turned them all down.

Andon did not care about wealth, though he had plenty. He did not care to live in a big city; his work drew his customers to him. He cared only about the making of what people referred to as Soulshards. These were unique swords for those with the ability to use them. Anyone with the proper skill could infuse a Shard with a piece of their animus. This allowed them to preserve their knowledge and skill and to pass it on to any Adept who held the blade.

Andon took a piece of strange, dark stone carved into a triangle. The triangle was the perfect size to fit the corresponding hole. The stone was very thin, thin enough to lay flat with the blade when it was set.

Andon took his time setting the piece of soulstone. This was the most delicate part of the process, and it took all of his concentration. When the stone was fitted into the hole, he used one hand to hold it in place while he took the forefinger of his free hand and ran it along the edge where the stone met steel. The place where the two objects met glowed with a soft white light, as he drew his finger along. His finger moved slowly; it took him almost two full minutes to complete the triangle. When he finished with the top side, he turned the blade over and repeated the process on the other side.

Andon sighed and took a seat. It was exhausting work to bind a piece of soulstone to a blade. The black triangle stood out from the clean steel like a blackened heart. But Andon knew that when someone bonded the blade, the stone would turn a pearlescent white.

Andon felt his eyes grow heavy and got to his feet before he could doze off. There was still work to be done. He had to fashion the hilt and decorate it according to the specifics of the order that his awaiting customer had placed. He was about to start when a soft knock sounded on the door to the smithy.

Andon turned in surprise. No one in town would be awake at this hour. He moved to the door, but did not open it.

"Who is there?" he called softly.

"An old friend," came the reply in a similarly soft voice, "on a desperate errand."

The voice was familiar, though Andon could not place it immediately. He opened the door and saw a small, thin man standing outside. He had long white hair and a long white beard. His bright eyes were shadowed by his heavy, arched eyebrows.

"Waylan?" Andon asked, almost incredulous. "Is that you? I haven't seen you in years!"

Andon motioned for the man to enter, but Waylan held up a hand.

"I'm afraid I need your help with something out here," the old man said. "I cannot carry him on my own." He turned and walked back toward the horse that stood by the road. A large man was slumped in the saddle. Andon hurried after Waylan and helped him carry the man inside. He closed the door behind them and bolted it; whatever Waylan wanted; Andon knew it would need to be private.

"Who is this?" Andon asked, eyeing the limp man. They had propped him in a sitting position against the wall near the fire. The firelight played across his features, giving Andon a good look at him. The man's hair was short and grey; his face was clean-shaven but scarred in many places. His left eye was covered by a patch, and his cheeks were sunken. He was tall and, at one point, must have been a broad, strong man. But now, he was as lean as a starved dog, and his skin was raw as if he had been in the sun for many days without cover. His chest moved slowly with shallow breaths.

"Are you familiar with the legends of Oren Tor?" Waylan asked. Andon nodded. Everyone knew Oren Tor. He was the first king of Bendel and the mightiest warrior anyone had ever seen. He had slayed a dragon and fought other strange, fell thing, at least, according to the legends. Also, according to the legends, he had disappeared after many years of prosperous rule. Waylan gestured to the limp man.

"Well, there he is," Waylan said with a sigh of grief.

"That's impossible!" Andon said. Oren Tor had lived almost a thousand years ago. There was no way this could be him. If he did not know Waylan better, he would be certain the man was conning him in some way.

But Andon did know Waylan. Not terribly well, but well enough to trust him.

"Unlikely," Waylan responded wearily, "but not impossible."

"Tell me," Andon said, "tell me how this could be him and what you want of me." He doubted he would be able to help. Whoever this man was, he needed a physicker or a mortician, not a smith.

"It is a long tale," Waylan said, "and even I do not know all of it." He settled himself on a stool by the work table. "A long time ago, I began…. recruiting, you could say. There is a conflict happening across many worlds, and I needed men with certain abilities to aid in it. Oren was one that agreed to join me."

"So, he didn't disappear all those years ago?"

"From this world, yes," Waylan answered. "But he did not vanish into some unknown void, no. He began to accomplish tasks for me. He visited different worlds and helped to keep things stable. To offset the chaos my adversary was attempting to unleash."

"And who is this 'adversary'?" Andon probed.

"I suppose you deserve to be told," Waylan sighed. "His name is Isar. Or at least, that is the name he uses most. We have opposing views on a few very crucial matters, and so we have striven against each other for many long years." Andon did not understand much of what Waylan was saying. There were more worlds than this one? And someone, this Isar, wanted to unleash chaos on them? It made very little sense to the smith.

"How did Oren, if this is Oren Tor, come to live so long? He disappeared almost a thousand years ago."

"The people I choose to help me receive certain benefits. Among them is an extended lifespan." Waylan fixed his bright blue eyes on Andon. "And he is Oren Tor. I swear it by oak and ash and elm. I swear it by the Yew-Slope itself." Andon was not sure what any of that swearing meant. They were not things he had ever heard anyone swear by. He was beginning to doubt how much he really knew Waylan. Or if he knew him at all.

"Very well, but how did Oren come to be in this state?"

"We have certain places where we meet. Oren was gone for a long time. Much longer than is typical. When he finally arrived, he was as you see him. Starved, weak, and wounded." Waylan walked over to the slumped form of Oren Tor. He pulled back the sleeve of Oren's right arm, baring it up to the shoulder. A black scar ran along his bicep. Thin black lines crept from the wound, spidering outward like a malevolent, poisonous web. "I have done what I can to keep him going, but this wound, whatever caused it, is beyond my skill to heal. Or anyone else's, I believe." It was the most horrifying wound Andon had ever seen. He could not imagine what might have caused it.

"So, what did Oren do for you, exactly?" Andon asked.

"Many things," Waylan looked at Andon as if considering something. "I would tell you if I could, but the tale would be even longer, and I fear time is limited for us." He gestured to where Oren sat, still unmoving.."

"And what would you have me do about that?" Andon said. "I have some skill in treating wounds, but I am no doctor."

"He does not need a doctor," Waylan said with a shake of his head. "He needs a Shard. An empty one." Andon looked at the fresh-forged sword lying on the table.

"I'm sorry, Waylan," Andon said, "but that sword is for someone else. They've already paid, and I cannot simply give it away. Ask anything else of me and it is yours. But I cannot renege on a customer."

"No," Waylan said with a dry chuckle, "I would not expect you to. And I do not want that blade. The one I need will be different. It will need to be a blade made entirely of soulstone. More of a carving than a forging." Andon was stunned. A sword made entirely of soulstone! It was unthinkable. The amount of money it would cost for a piece of stone that big and the time it would take to carve it was both absurd.

"Waylan, that is simply an untenable request," Andon answered after a moment of stunned silence. "I wouldn't begin to guess where to find that much soulstone, or how long it would take to carve it."

"Take as much time as you need, so long as you work as quickly as you can. I will keep him alive for as long as it takes. I have already put him into a trance to slow the poison," Waylan said. "As to the soulstone, it is a non-issue." He walked out of the smithy and returned a few moments later, carrying the largest piece of soulstone that Andon had ever seen. It was almost too big for Waylan to carry. Nearly four feet long and a foot thick, it must have weighed at least six or seven stone.

"Where did you get that?" Andon asked, incredulous. "That must be more soulstone than exists in all the world!"

"At least," Waylan agreed. "As to how I got it, it is immaterial. I have it, and that is what matters." He looked at Andon steadily. "Will you help me? You are the only smith on Trallis with the skill to do this." Andon sighed. It was no choice at all.

"Of course, I will help if you truly believe that this will work. But it will take me days to carve this properly."

"Do what you must," Waylan said, "and will do my best to keep Oren alive to do his part. May the Nine watch over us."

Andon wasn't sure what he meant by the 'nine'. If they were gods of some kind, he had never heard of them. Andon was not a religious man, but the only religion he knew anything about was the zealots who worshipped Sha, the One God. It made no difference to Andon what a man believed, so long as they didn't ask him to get involved.

Andon took the mass of stone from Waylan and set it on the work table. He gathered his tools for carving soulstone; it required a very particular sort of chisel and a careful touch on the hammer. He set to work, knowing time was scarce, but also knowing that great work could not be rushed. He had promised to help, but he had significant doubts about Oren living long enough to do whatever Waylan expected him to do.

It took three days to make the blade. Andon would never have believed he could have done it so quickly, especially without any sleep. Each time his eyes grew heavy and he felt he would need a rest; Waylan would lay his hand on Andon's shoulder and a fresh reserve of energy would flood into him. It did not even occur to him until the job was nearly done that he had not stopped once. He did not sleep, he did not eat, and he did not see a single person other than Waylan and Oren. There was no talking while he worked. Waylan treated his patient in silence and kept the forge fire burning. Other than that, time seemed to hardly move at all.

At the end of the third day, Andon stood, his muscles complaining at the sudden stretch. He looked down at the finely crafted blade of dark stone. It was almost three feet of blade, with a half-foot of tang to be fitted to a hilt. Pride welled up in Andon that he had made such a fine thing, even as he doubted how it might be ed. Waylan moved to stand at his side, ing down at the sword.

"You have done well," Waylan said, resting his hand on Andon's mighty shoulder. "It is as fine a thing as I have ever seen made." Andon flushed at the praise but was too tired to do more than nod his acceptance of the adulation.

"Well," Waylan said, "it is time to wake our friend up and hope he has the strength to do what he must." He moved over to where Oren had remained slumped against the wall for the past three days. His condition did not seem much changed, other than his skin was paler, and his one eye flickered restlessly beneath its lid.

Waylan laid his hand on Oren's forehead and spoke softly. Andon could not hear what he said, but the effect was immediate.

Oren startled awake and would have cried out if Waylan had not pressed his hand to Oren's lips. Oren's eye found Waylan's and he calmed a bit.

"Wh-Wh-Where…am…I?" his voice rasped in his throat. He coughed slightly, sweat breaking out on his forehead.

"You are safe," Waylan told him soothingly, "but it is time for you to pass on. I cannot do anything for your wounds. You don't have much time. Do you think you have the strength?"

Oren's eyes searched the room and seemed to lock on the sword of soulstone lying on the table.

"So," he said with another cough, "it's time at last."

"We knew it would come," Waylan said, sadly, "ever since the mists." Oren nodded.

"Bring it here." Andon obeyed wordlessly, bringing the blade over to the dying man. His skin was already greyer than it had been, and his one eye was clouded with pain. Andon offered it to Oren, the tang held out for him to grasp.

Oren reached out his hand and grasped the thin piece of soulstone that would soon be bound in a hilt. His eye grew distant, and his body trembled. Light began to seep from his hand into the stone sword. It grew through the stone in tiny webs of lights; thin lines of pearlescent white boring through the darkness of the stone. It went on longer than any bonding Andon had ever seen, but finally, Oren's hand went limp and fell from the sword.

The lined of white had grown thicker and thicker, and even now, when Oren was no longer touching it, they continued to widen and lengthen until the entire blasé shone with white light. When all the stone had been consumed by white, the blade gave off a faint ringing, like a distant bell. The light faded, leaving a pale, milky white color permeating the entire sword. Without a sound, Oren's body went rigid and tipped to the side, collapsing to the floor.

Andon stared in shock. This was beyond any soul-forging he had ever seen.

"How much of his animus did he give to the blade?" he asked, although he thought he already knew the answer.

"All of it," Waylan answered. "He gave it all."

A New Purpose

Fel Narnir followed the twisting stone cavern, deeper and deeper into the mountain. He could not help the unease he felt as he went further in; there was something…different about this place. The air felt heavy, and the mists that hung above him, obscuring the ceiling of the caverncavern's ceiling, were deeply profoundly unnatural. There seemed to be images in the mist, but Kalas had warned him about this so he did his best to ignore them. There was an eerie light thatAn eerie light seemed to come from no source, lighting the way forward just enough to see by. His lank, brown hair was beginning to mat to his forehead as sweat broke from his skin.

Fel was not entirely sure why he was here. Kalas had told him how to get here and assured him he would be safe, but Fel still questioned whether this was his best option. He couldn't stay in Napel, of course; not with Ashanar and Tyra there. But there were plenty of other places in the world he could go. Still, he could not deny that he was curious. Kalas had said he could find a new purpose here. A use for his powers that could redeem all the awful things he had done. For that reason, he had sailed north and crossed the whole of the Weldoran to be here.

The passage narrowed until Fel was almost touching the walls with each shoulder. The downward slope had gotten steeper, and he almost lost his balance several times. The light began to dim until, at last, the floor leveled out abruptly, and the passage turned sharply to the right. He stepped into a room brightly lit by the same source less glow. It was an enormous cavern, made of smooth, dark stone. At the center of the room, a stone arch stood, lit by a dim blue light.

There were a few alcoves set in the walls of the caverncavern's walls, though they were too dark for Fel to see whether there was anything in them. The dark stone of the walls was as smooth as glass, and had thin veins of sliver running through it. He walked over toward one of the walls, tracing one of the lines with his finger.

"Where did this come from?" Fel wondered aloud; , a muttered thought that was barely audible, even to his own ears. Yet, he received an answer.

"Another world." The voice came from behind Fel, causing him to spin around in alarm. Standing on the opposite side of the cavern, which had certainly undoubtedly been empty seconds ago, was a small man. He was perhaps five feet tall, but only just. He had long, white hair, pulled back from his long, narrow face. His thick, snowy eyebrows hung heavy over a pair of deep green eyes and had an unusual sharpness at the corners. His eyes were very oldancient, though Fel was not sure why he knew that was so.

"I did not think you would come, Son of Solus," the old man said, "but since you have, let us begin."

"Begin what?" Fel asked, suspiciously. "Who are you?"

"Your new path," the old man said. "A chance to find a new purpose for your life. As for my name, you may call me Waylan." Fel did not like the first answer. It was just like what Kalas had told him, and he was tired of the vague answers.

"What does all that mean? A new purpose?" Fel asked, his patience growing thin.

"And what did you mean by 'another world?'" The old man stared at him, blankly. He stroked his beard and shook his head.

"Did Kalas tell you nothing?" Waylan asked, almost incredulously.

"Very little," Fel responded. "All he told me before he died was how to find this place and that I could find a new direction for my life here." Waylan's eyes widened in sudden shock.

"Kalas is dead?" Waylan said as if it was impossible.

"Yes, he died weeks ago." ," Fel was surprised. "You didn't know?"

"No," Waylan said. "I did not." He turned away from Fel and began to pace around the chamber. "Oh, that is a blow against us." This news seemed deeply troubling to the old man, but Fel could not tell why. Who was this man, and what had Kalas had to do with him?

"Will you just tell me why I'm here?" Fel asked, his impatience overriding any sense of respect for the old man's apparent grief. Waylan looked at him with something close to anger, but he masked it quickly.

"Yes, I suppose that is only fair," Waylan allowed. "The time will come later for mourning Kalas. And all the others we've lost as well." He resumed stroking his beard, considering what to say next.

"Have you ever looked up at the stars and wondered about what other worlds might be out there? Have you ever thought about your place in the larger universe?" Waylan asked these things as if he already knew thatknew Fel had had these thoughts many times. "Have you ever wondered about the gods and whether they truly exist?" Fel nodded but could not find any words to add. The old man eyed him critically. "Well, I can answer these questions and more. If Kalas sent you to me, he must have known you were an able candidate to replace him."

"Replace him how?" Waylan waved the question away.

"All in due time," the old man said. "If I am to explain things right, I must start at the beginning." Waylan settled himself cross-legged on the ground. He indicated that Fel should do the same. "First, you must learn that the gods are real. Or, they were. They have been gone for a long time now. They created ten worlds with their incredible but not indefinite power. They created all the life that inhabits these worlds, both your kind and mine. But, the cost of these creations was the lives of the very gods themselves. With each world created, the gods had to give up something of themselves, something that we call a Spark. Each world has one of these Sparks, and it is these that power and sustain all life in existence."

"What do you mean 'my kind and your kind'?" Fel asked. "Are you not a man?"

"No, I am not one of your kind," Waylan said with a sighsighed. "My kind go go by all sorts of names, but the most common one is the Fae. We used to inhabit the mortal worlds, but we have long since moved to a realm of our own. A place called the Fael." He closed his eyes, and his body began to change. He grew taller and thinner, his skin turned golden, and long, pointed ears poke poked through is his white hair.

Fel stared in shock. Not just at the change in appearance but at the manner of the change. This was magic unlike any that Fel had seen or used. There had been no mist rising from Waylan to show what Essence he was drawing upon for his glamour. Fel was baffled.

Waylan closed his eyes again and returned to the form of an old man. He gave a half smile at Fel's shocked appearance.

"My kind have have many gifts." He said it as if that was all the explanation that Fel would need. "We can discuss that more later. For now, let me continue on with my tale." Waylan resettled himself on the ground and continued.

"There was another group of beings, called Arenai. These beings served the gods. But, one of them grew greedy for power. While the gods were busy with their creations, this Aren, Asha'tamenar'ash, found ways to grow in power." Waylan shook his head sadly. "We still do not know how he managed this, but we know it involved destroying other Arenai. Some few are left, but we do not know where they are and they cannot be relied upon."

"Asha'tamenar'ash used his newfound power to create his own world. He succeeded, in a way. He could not create life in the manner of our two kinds, but he managed to create many dark and dangerous things of his own. The home of his abominations we named Neth Gellin."

"When the gods realized what Asha'tamenar'ash was doing, they used almost all their remaining power to fence Asha'tamenar'ash and all his monstrosities in Neth Gellin. They are trapped there forever. This massive expense of power left the gods very weak, and so, in order to keep their creations alive, they gave up their remaining power into the last of the ten worlds; a place called Olthos. This land has no Spark, but it is filled with the last of the gods' power. That is all that sustains it."

"AlrightAll right," Fel said. "But, what does any of this have to do with me? Or Kalas?"

"What it has to do with you and Kalas and many others besides, is that there is a war raging on right now. Not the petty squabbling of one kingdom against another on one world or another. This is a conflict of small but important deeds. I have gathered powerful people from across the ten worlds to aid me in my goals."

"And what are those goals, exactly?" Fel prodded. "And who are we opposing? And what do they want?" Every answer Waylan gave seemed to spawn three new questions.

"My goals are simple," Waylan answered with just a touch of impatience. "To keep the Sparks safe and to ensure that the ten worlds continue to exist." He looked down at his folded hands. When he looked up again, his face was dark with anger. "As to who opposes us? He goes by the name Isar. He seeks to obtain the Sparks of each world. In furtherance of this goal, he also recruits mortals, like myself, but he uses them to sow discord among the worlds. He starts wars and undermines order and stability wherever he can."

"So, he just wants the power of these Sparks for himself?" Fel was disappointed that such beings could be so petty in their desires.

"Not for himself, no," Waylan said. "No, he believes that if he can free the power from the Sparks themselves, then he can revive the gods."

"And could he do it?" Fel asked. "Is it possible to bring them back?"

"Honestly," Waylan shook his head. "I do not know. Perhaps, he could. But it would come at the expense of all life in the ten worlds."

Waylan nodded to himself. "It certainly could be possible. But the gods charged us with protecting all life whenever we could. It would go against their love for their creations to do what Isar wants to do."

"It is also possible," Waylan added. "That the release of the Sparks' power could render everything else that power is used for useless. It could weaken or even allow the fences of Neth Gellin to fail. Who can say what madness would descend on the universe if that happened?"

"So, if I joined you," Fel said. "What exactly would that entail?"

"I will not lie," Waylan met his eyes with a hard look. "It will not be easy. I will send you to new and probably dangerous places. Sometimes alone and sometimes with other agents of mine." He smiled at Fel; it was a strange smile, like he knew he had Fel where he wanted him. "It will also allow you to go places and see things that few others ever will. You will have access to knowledge and powers beyond almost any other mortal."

Fel considered this. Power, for power's sake, had never held the appeal that his father and half-brother had sought. But that did not mean that Fel did not want to be stronger. He had always had someone stronger than himself giving orders. He had been forced to do things he would not have done on his own, though it had taken most of his life before he had realized how little he liked the things his father had asked of him. This was a chance to do something that would not only matter, but also allow him to live a new life. Honestly, there was nothing more to consider. His mind was made up.

"How do we begin?" Fel asked. Waylan looked at him with a touch of surprise. Obviously, he had been expecting to have to make a stronger more substantial sell.

"The first thing to do is to send you through the Waypoint." Waylan gestured to the stone archway behind him. "You must go to Atantris before doing anything else. There are many things you must learn thereYou must learn many things before you can freely use the Waypoints, which is, unfortunately, a necessity for our purposes."

"Atantris? I have never heard of that place."

"Atantris is the capital city of the Fael. And there will be many more places that I send you that you have never heard of. You have lived a short, sheltered life in comparison to what lays ahead."

"And what of this Isar person? Will he attempt to stop us?"

Waylan's eyes took on a distant look, as if he was seeing something far away. "As for Isar, he and I cannot actively oppose or hinder each other. A Covenant was made that forbids us from fighting or harming each other. However, he will likely send agents of his own to obstruct us where he may." Waylan walked up to Fel and placed two fingers against Fel's forehead. He closed his eyes, and Fel felt some kind of power flowing through him. "You have a strong animus, and you have mastered this world's forms of Expulsion and Absorption. But there are many more magics out there. It would behoove you to study them while you are in Atantris."

Waylan gestured again to the Waypoint. "It is time to go now. I will send you through to Fael and when you arrive, you must ask for a friend of mine, a Fae named Corlanis. He will show you around and help you to find the things you need to study. He will also contact me when you are ready to do more."

"Wait," Fel said in sudden alarm. "You aren't coming to Atantris with me?"

"No," Waylan had a sad look on his face. "Unfortunately, part of the Covenant prevents me from returning to the Fael,." He studied Fel's face for a moment. "Be patient in your studies. Time passes differently in the Fael. It will feel like a long time for you. But the skills and knowledge you will obtain there are necessary to the thingswhat I will ask of you in the future." He turned and walked toward the stone archway. He reached forward and touched the bluish light in the center of the arch. The light turned a bright white and expanded to fill the archway. "It is time. When you arrive, you will find yourself in a grove of trees just outside the city. Remember, the first thing you must do is find Corlanis." He nodded to Fel and gestured toward the portal of light.

Fel walked slowly toward the shining doorway. He was nervous. What if this was all some elaborate lie? What if this portal killed him? Or trapped him somewhere? No, he told himself. The time for doubt was behind him. Kalas had sent him here and Fel had made his choice. He would follow through with this new purpose.

Fel stepped into the light. He felt a very disorienting spinning sensation that ended with him stumbling onto a sward of brilliant green grass. He was in a clearing of elm trees. The air was full of life in a way he had never experienced. Colors were sharper, smells; smells were strongerstronger more pungent; even the very air felt more alive. He looked to the north and saw massive shapes rising over the trees. They were towers made of some strange stone.

No, not stone. Glass. Countless towers of shining, colorful glass stood out against the clearest, bluest sky he had ever seen.

Fel took a deep breath. The air filling him made him feel more alive than he had ever felt before. He felt powerful and free in ways that almost defied description.

Fel decided he could most definitely enjoy his time in this strange, wonderful place. He strode forward toward the edge of the clearing with the glass towers to guide him in the direction of the city.

Fel walked with purpose and confidence toward his new life.

The Waypoint

The Nameless One stared out from the prow of the rowboat as its oars pulled them closer and closer to the mist-shrouded shores ahead. He was not truly Nameless; it had been hundreds of years since the Sha'mor had lost whatever power it was that had given them the ability to scour their leader's name from all living memory. But the tradition of the title remained. Some claimed that they had committed some sin or failed in some way, earning Sha's wrath. Surely, only that could account for the loss of their power and the rapid waning of their influence in the lands of men.

The leaders of the Free Lands no longer looked to the Priests of Sha for guidance. The common people no longer feared the wrath or punishment of the One God. Fewer and fewer initiates came every year, and now the Faithful numbered in the dozens where once it had been thousands. Sha'an was a shell of its former glory. The Temple was falling into disrepair, a brutal, although fitting analogy for the corruption growing in the souls of the world's people.

Despite all this, the Nameless One could not bear to break with tradition and allow his underlings to address him by, or even acknowledge they remembered his true name. In his ten years as the leader of the Sha'mor, not one person had uttered the name Alanor. He appreciated their dedication, these last few faithful followers. They had followed him in his fight to try to restore Sha's name and glory. And they had followed him here, driven only by a dream.

The dream came just over a month ago. A man, older with close-cropped greying hair and a short grey beard, had spoken to Alanor and told him to undertake this journey. His green eyes had shone as he'd spoken to Alanor of how Sha's glory might be restored. Of how Alanor might return the souls of an entire world to the True Path.

But first, this journey. A journey very few mortals had ever undertaken, and even fewer had survived.

The first rowboat touched the shore, oarsmen hopping out to pull the boats up out of the surf. The others soon followed, and in time, the forty or so left of the Sha'mor, along with their accompanying guardsmen, were arrayed on the edge of the forested hills that led deeper onto the island. Mist swirled above the trees, obscuring whatever lay beyond.

Alanor felt fear rising in him. They had made it this far, but the reputation of this place, the myths and legends that spoke of the horrors that awaited any mortal who proceeded further, pushed themselves to the front of his mind.

And then he saw the man from his dream. The man's face was, as he remembered, greyhaired and grey bearded with eyes as green as summer grass. He was tall and strong looking, clothed in robes of black. He seemed like a warrior-priest of old, a living legend.

Alanor approached the man, with a mixture of awe and fear. Something about this man radiated power. Standing in his presence was just as it had felt in the dream. Surely, this man must be a servant of Sha.

"I have come as you instructed," Alanor said, bowing his head in a show of respect. The man looked him up and down, his dark eyes were hard chips of onyx set in his weathered face. He turned his gaze upon the rest of Alanor's group.

"This is all you have brought?" the man asked. "I was hoping for more."

"This is all that remains of the true followers of our Lord," Alanor replied. He hesitated before continuing. "If I might ask, who are you, and how did you come to be here?" Alanor had many more questions, but for the moment, he held them in. The man's eyes found Alanor again, his mouth set in a frown.

"I am called Isar, and I am here because I am needed." He turned and began walking back toward the woods. Alanor followed quickly, although it was challenging to keep up with Isar's quick gait in his robes. Isar did not slow until he reached the tree line. He looked over his shoulder at Alanor as he struggled up the hill. The trees before them were a mix of all kinds. Oak, elm, ash, yew, and others he could not identify. Several yards into their midst, the mist obscured everything.

"Call your people forward, priest," Isar told him. "I must speak to them all before we proceed." He turned to the trees, staring forward as if contemplating something difficult.

Alanor was not sure what to make of this. This strange man commanded him as if he were not the leader of the True Path! He had even called Alanor "priest" as if he were some ordinary man. Only the memory of his dream, and the strangeness of this entire enterprise, kept him from objecting.

Alanor turned and signaled for the rest of the party to proceed, then turned to face Isar.

"What exactly are we proceeding with?" Alanor asked. Isar eyed him without turning his head before responding.

"I told you in your dream. We are here to resurrect your dying religion. To give you power again. In order to do that, we must follow a path that few of your kind have ever followed before." Isar turned his attention back to the misty forest. Alanor could not see what was so fascinating about it, although the mist had a certain disconcerting quality to it.

"Yes, but how exactly are we to do that? Your message was rather vague on how we are to accomplish these mighty things."

"All will be told when we reach the Temple." A touch of irritation tainted Isar's voice. "Those of you that survive, at least."

The flat tone with which Isar delivered this last comment deeply unnerved Alanor. What kind of peril had he put his people in? What truly waited in those mists?

The sound of feet roused Alanor from his contemplation. He turned and saw that his followers had reached the top of the rise and now waited for whatever was to come next. Isar also turned regarding the people assembled before him as a man might observe a shed full of tools. His expression clearly showed that he did not find these tools particularly impressive.

"Followers of Sha!" Isar said, raising his voice to be heard by all. "You have completed a great journey in the name of your God. But, you have further yet to go." He looked around intently. "Much further." Some priests shuffled their feet or looked to their comrades, clearly uneasy with this stranger who suddenly appeared to be in charge. Alanor could not help but share their discomfiture.

"Through this forest lies a temple," Isar continued. "That temple is our destination. In that temple is the key to regaining your lost power and influence." He looked at Alanor as if he could seethrough him, into his skin, and down to the very marrow of his bones. It was a disturbing experience for Alanor. But he could not deny that he desired what Isar promised more than anything else.

"Unfortunately, there is one obstacle remaining to your quest. The mists you see that cover this land; they are more than a simple haze. As you travel through them, you will encounter visions. Some of the past, some of the future. They may horrify you, they may give you strength, or they may simply drive you mad."

Isar looked around again, appraisingly. The gathered priests seemed deeply unsettled by his words, but none had turned aside yet.

"Those of you who make it through will be rewarded." Isar went on. "Those who do not, will be remembered. The future of your religion begins today." Without another word, Isar strode forward into the trees, quickly disappearing into the mists.

Alanor hesitated briefly. His men needed to see he was not afraid. They needed his leadership now more than ever. Besides, they were just visions. They would not be harmed in flesh, knowing that should be enough to keep them going.

"You heard him!" Alanor shouted to the Sha'mor. "We must go onward. Keep faith in our Lord Sha and in the True Path, which has led us here." With that, he turned and followed Isar's example, striding purposefully into the mists.

The mists immediately obscured anything more than several feet away from Alanor. He looked behind himself, but could not see anything other than the shadows of trees. Had his men forsaken him? Had they let their fear overcome their duty to Sha?

It did not matter, Alanor decided. Even if he were the only one that forged on, he would do as he had set out to do and bring back the might of the One True God.

The mists disoriented Alanor to the point that he was not even sure he was headed toward the center of the island anymore. He walked on and on, barely keeping from bumping into trees.

The mists never lessened, and each stretch of several feet looked and felt the same as all the others. He could not say how long he had been walking. It could have been one hour or many, when the trees began to lessen. He excitedly moved forward, increasing his pace in the hopes he was almost free of this unnatural haze.

Alanor suddenly stumbled into an open area. The mists were gone, but the grass beneath his feat had vanished as soon as he was clear of the trees. He was standing in a barren land;withered trees and rocky ground were all he could see. Before he had the chance to wonder at this too much, a massive creature appeared before him. It had the body of a man, but the head of a wolf. A wicked-looking axe was clutched in its hands. It raised the axe and swung it at him with a ferocity that he had never encountered in his life.

Alanor fell back screaming as the creature's weapon missed him by less than a hand's breadth. As he fell on his back, the area around him exploded into life. Men dressed for war were all around. More wolf-headed creatures appeared, and the two groups began to hack at each other. Blood flowed like rivers of red across the broken, dead ground. Men died screaming, bodies hewn cruelly by the massive weapons wielded by the horrid beast-men. Several small groups of men managed to team up to overwhelm individual creatures, but it was clear the men could not stand long against such monsters.

Alanor did the only thing he could think to do. He ran, head down, doing his best to avoid the violence. Some small part of him remembered Isar's warning about the visions. But the greater part was too overcome by terror to let logic rule him. As he ran, the sounds of the battle faded, and the mists returned.

Alanor found himself among the shrouded trees again, bending over almost double to catch his breath and calm his racing heart. His thoughts became clearer, and he decided that the vision must have been one of those Isar had said that was meant to drive men mad. Surely, no such thing had ever, or could ever, happen in the real world.

Alanor trudged along through the mists again. He was growing weary of the monotonous sights of hazy tree shapes, when he was suddenly free of the mists again. This time, he found himself in some massive cavern. Ice hung from the ceiling in great spikes, like teeth hanging from the maw of some fearsome beast. He contemplated where he should go when he realized he was not alone in the cavern.

An old man, tall and lean, knelt at the far end of the massive chamber of rock and ice. The man's hair and beard were pure white. The hair of his head hung halfway down his back, and the beard was almost to his belt. Both were unkempt and wild. A scar ran along his jaw, almost from his ear to his chin. He seemed to be scraping at the frozen ground and muttering to himself.

Alanor approached the stranger slowly. As he got closer, he saw an old leatherbound book lying beside the man. The man's hands were raw and bleeding from tearing at the hard earth.

"Done what I can…. all that I can," the man was muttering. "Decieved… we were all deceived…. liar, he lied, always lies."

The man was clearly mad, Alanor decided. But he was unable to tear his attention away from the stranger. The man finally seemed satisfied with his digging. Alanor peered over his shoulder to see the small pit the madman had dug. It was shallow, less than half a foot deep. But apparently, it was all the man needed.

"The truth must remain… only way to end the lies."

The man lifted the small book, pressed his lips to it and placed it in the hole. He scraped the hard dirt back over the hole and patted it down. He let out a great sigh and pitched over sideways.

Alanor was startled by the sudden sharp movement. He was about to move forward to see if he could help the man, but at that moment, he noticed a mist had begun to rise from the ground to his right. Somehow, he knew that this was his way out of the vision. He walked into the mist and found himself again in the shrouded woods.

Heartened now that not all these visions would be of chaos and violence, even if there was no discernable meaning to them, Alanor forged forward through the trees.

On and on, Alanor went until the mists began to fade again. He hurried forward, hoping his ordeal might be done.

Instead, Alanor found himself standing on a massive white stone bridge amid a massive city. The city was made of all white stone, just like the bridge. Ten towers stood around the city, stars shone in the night sky overhead, and singing could be heard wafting through the air. It felt peaceful.

But it did not last.

The air was rent by screams of terror. Fires sprang up among the buildings of the city. People were running everywhere, pursued by groups of assailants. The assailants' garb was unusual. They wore grey robes belted by rope, and they carried weapons. He watched as the grey-robed attackers slaughtered the city's inhabitants. It was sickening, but worse was to come.

Alanor noticed, out of the corner of his eye, that one of the mighty towers had fallen. No fire had touched it and no great engines of war were in evidence. Yet the tower had crumbled and collapsed. One by one, the other towers followed suit until none remained standing.

A group of fleeing refugees came running up the span of the great bridge upon which

Alanor stood. As they passed him, he saw their pursuers up close. At their head was a man all in white; white robe, white belt, holding a staff of white. His long white beard flowed over his shoulder as he ran, long white hair billowing behind him. Something about the man's face seemed familiar, though Alanor could not place it. Both groups soon passed him by; he was too stunned to run or try to otherwise intervene in the horrific scene around him.

A new figure caught Alanor's attention as it approached the bridge. It was built like a man, but robed all in black with its cowl drawn down over its face. It raised a pale, ghostlike hand, and the bridge around Alanor was engulfed in black flame.

Alanor found himself back in the misty woods, shaking and sweating. What horror had he just witnessed? Was that past or future? Or just some strange terror meant to break his mind? He shook his head; he doubted if he would ever know.

After a few minutes spent recovering, Alanor continued. He entered and endured several more visions, each coming and going more quickly than the ones before. He witnessed nine stars fall from the sky, streaking across the firmament like bolts of bluish fire. He observed nine flames rise from the earth and come together to create a massive conflagration that burned like the sun. He saw many other things that he could not put into words. Vision after vision until, at last, he stumbled into a clearing of clean, green grass. The mists swirled around the edge of the clearing, but did not enter it.

Alanor was unsure if he was in a new vision until he looked up at the massive stone structure that stood in the middle of the clearing. It was a great mass of pure white stone; towers rose from each corner and a series of great steps led up to the front doors of the building.

Sitting on those steps, was Isar.

Alanor was sure now that he had reached the Temple. He started toward Isar when he noticed other people in the clearing. They seemed to have emerged from the mists at the same time as he did. Many of them lay on the ground, groaning or lying silent. Obviously, they had not fared as well as Alanor had.

Isar rose and descended the steps. He walked around the clearing, going to each man and touching a finger to their foreheads. Some of those he touched rose slowly, others lay still. A few others sat up and babbled incoherently, muttering to themselves, much like the strange old man from Alanor's vision.

When Isar was finished, only about thirty of the priests seemed to be in decent shape and about an equal number of their guards. The rest were either unconscious, dead, or undeniably mad.

"Come," Isar said, without preamble, as he reached Alanor. "We still have much to do."

Alanor wanted to protest; his men needed rest, and Alanor himself wanted an explanation as to what would be done with those unable to continue. But, before he could voice his objections, he noticed the rest of the survivors were already moving towards the Temple. They moved as if caught in a dreamlike trance. Alanor decided he could do no more than follow suit.

Isar led them into the Temple, then down through winding corridors and steep, narrow staircases. The walls of white stone were decorated in carved images. It was too dark and they proceeded too fast for Alanor to puzzle out what they depicted.

They descended what must have been hundreds of feet below ground. At last, they reached a room at what felt like the depths of the world. The room was circular in shape and unlit, except for the light that emanated from a large stone archway that stood in the center of the room. An odd, bluish light came from the center of the arch. Alanor could not guess what this thing might be, but he could feel the power that vibrated through the air of the chamber.

"What is this place?" Alanor asked, his voice seemed jarring in the otherwise silent chamber.

"It is called a Waypoint." Isar looked at Alanor with that piercing stare. "It is how you will journey to new worlds in order to bring Sha's glory to those who need it." Alanor was stunned. New worlds? That was not what he had been promised. He opened his mouth to argue, but Isar cut him off.

"Olthos is lost to the truth. You must move on if the True Path is to survive." Isar stared at Alanor, waiting for him to respond.

Ultimately, Alanor could do nothing more than nod. He was exhausted from his ordeal in the mists and could hardly wrap his mind around the concept of other worlds. But if this was the only way to save the Sha'mor, he would take it.

Isar began to break the remaining priests into groups of three or four, assigning a few guards to each group. They then reached forward and touched the source of the light that came from the arch. The light turned a deeper blue before bursting into clear, white light. The groups that Isar had designated began to walk through the arch; each group disappeared as they stepped through.

Finally, Alanor was left with Isar, two other priests, and three guards. Alanor alone seemed perturbed by what had just occurred. Where had the rest of them gone?

"Your turn," Isar said, turning to Alanor and the others. The remaining priests and guards strode forward without hesitation as if under some spell. They passed through the arch and disappeared, just like all the rest.

"Come along," Isar said, his dark eyes holding Alanor's gaze.

"Where does it lead?"

"To a new world. A new world, ripe for your guidance."

Alanor wanted to protest, to argue that this was not what had been promised. But something about Isar's gaze made it clear he would brook no disagreements.

Alanor strode up to the arch and, after a moment's hesitation, stepped through. He felt as though the whole world fell away behind him. He was spinning through some unknown ether, tetherless, unbound.

At last, Alanor found himself falling forward through an arch similar to the one he had just stepped through. He was standing in an enormous stone cavern. The cavern was filled with strange crystals. They grew from the ground and sprouted from the walls. They came in all manner of colors, and there seemed no rhyme nor reason as to why each color grew where.

The other priests and guards from that final group also stood in the chamber. They stared around in the same sort of awe that Alanor himself felt. Alanor felt a hand on his shoulder, startling him out of his reverie, as Isar came through the arch and pushed past Alanor.

Isar strode to the center of the chamber and looked up toward the ceiling. Alanor then noticed that there was a balcony of a sort there. And standing on that balcony was a man. The man was old, long white hair hung past his shoulders. His face was thin and clean-shaven. His eyes were the brightest green that Alanor had ever seen in a person. He was tall and thin, and held a staff of some strange wood in his right hand.

"You cannot be here, Isar," the old man said, his voice ringing through the chamber.

"There is no such prohibition, Reuel," Isar returned simply. "Except perhaps by Waylan, but we both know he is not the authority he pretends to be."

The old man seemed to consider these words, then turned and silently walked away from the edge of the balcony. Isar beckoned to Alanor and the others and walked toward the far end of the chamber. A doorway was carved into the rocky wall and led to a set of stairs that spiraled upward.

Alanor and the others followed Isar up the stairs for a long time until they emerged into a grand entry hall of some kind. Nine alcoves were carved into the walls of the hall, and each cavity held a massive carved figure. Alanor would have preferred to spend some time studying these things, but Isar hurried them toward the enormous pair of doors at the end of the hall.

"This world has never known the touch of Sha, or your True Path," Isar said to Alanor as they stood before the great doors. "It will be your duty to bring them the Truth." He handed Alanor a book. It was black leatherbound and thick. "This will help you find the power you need to do your God's will."

Alanor noticed for the first time that Isar referred to Sha as "your" God, not "our" God. For the first time since the mists, he found the will to question this strange man.

"Why did you bring us here? What do you get out of this?" Alanor asked.

"You needed help," Isar responded blandly, "and I believe in helping those who need it." He smiled an odd small smile, "And someday, I may need your help. I trust that you will be willing to answer my call when that time comes."

"Perhaps," Alanor hedged, not wanting to commit anything to this strange man. "What kind of help would you need from us? And where are the rest of my followers?" The second question had just occurred to him.

"Nothing that your God would object to," Isar said, answering my first question with that same small grin. "As to where your followers have gone? They have been sent to other places. To help further spread the word of your Lord Sha."

"Now, no further questions," Isar continued, "I must return, and it is time you brought the True Path to the world of Aeros." Without further explanation, he pushed on the massive doors, which swung open as easily as a well-oiled simple oak door. Alanor was caught staring at the expanse of the snowy valley beyond the doors, and when he thought to turn back, Isar was already disappearing down the stairs back toward the crystal chamber.

"Well, my brothers," Alanor said, looking at his remaining brethren, "let us do as our strange friend says. Let us bring the True Path to this new world for the glory of Sha."

With that, the small group walked out into a new world.

A Sea of Sand

It was dark in the library except for the solitary candle that lit the table where Alhud sat, reading a book. The book was called The Glimpse. It had been written by a madman named Arac. Arac claimed that he had visited a land of mist and seen the future there. It was considered by most scholars to be utterly worthless.

But, Alhud was not most scholars. He was not actually a scholar at all, but a slave. His master, one of Noem's most powerful guild-masters, was named Janus Obari. Obari was a rare form of slave master. He looked for more in a slave than a strong back. This was not to say that Alhud did not perform physical labor; he worked all day in the sun alongside his fellow captives. But his nights he was allowed to spend in the library.

Alhud had been born free, a child to relatively wealthy parents, in distant M'barra. He had an excellent education and quickly proved to possess a sharp mind. He was only fifteen when the Noemi invaded his home. They were not there to conquer, simply to raid; they took what they could and fled. This included people. Noem had built its mighty empire on the backs of millions of slaves.

When Alhud had been sold to Obari, he was put to work building the guild-master's new palace. In the course of the work, he had pointed out to one of the overseers that the workers could be deployed more efficiently. This was an important observation as the work had been behind schedule at the time and Obari was not pleased. When word reached Obari of his clever new slave, he summoned Alhud and questioned him. He was delighted by Alhud's mind and offered him use of the library to continue his education. All Obari asked in return was that Alhud occasionally use his time researching things for his master. Alhud had agreed immediately.

And so, ten years later, Alhud found himself in the library, reading this madman's book because Obari was interested in it. Apparently, some disturbing signs had been seen lately, things that pointed to the possibility of Arac's prophecies being correct.

Yet, so far, the book seemed nothing more than the ravings of a lunatic. Arac spoke of strange things; a mighty serpent's nest pulled apart by ants, a golden triangle burning in the night, a pale prince commanding a sea in storm. It all sounded like nonsense to Alhud.

He sat back in his chair with a sigh, the light from his candle dancing across his dark skin. He ran his hand over his shaved head and rubbed at his heavy eyes. He wanted to give it up and return to the shack he shared with several other slaves, but he dared not until he finished reading Arac's drivel.

The sound of one of the library's heavy stone doors opening startled Alhud to alertness. It was rare that he was disturbed here. The sound of heavy footsteps walking through the stacks told Alhud that it must be one of the guards. And sure enough, one of Obari's guards appeared, carrying a lantern. He approached Alhud's table stoically.

"New arrivals coming in," the guard said. "The Master wants you to deal with them."

This was strange, but Alhud knew better than to argue, so he nodded his head, closed the book, and picked up his candle. He followed the guard out of the library and through the massive palace halls. It was not unusual for Obari to have Alhud help the new slaves adjust. But it was almost unheard of for a new batch to come in at night. They exited the palace and got into a donkey-led cart that was waiting for them. It was a short ride to the harbor, which was where most arrivals came in.

There were many ships at anchor in the massive harbor, but only one was currently unloading. Alhud got out of the cart and watched the ship, waiting to see how many new slaves he would be spending his night looking after. It could not be many, as they had brought just one cart.

Alhud was shocked when a single man, hands and feet bound in shackles, was led down the gangplank. The man had a hood over his head, obscuring Alhud's vision of his face.

"That's the one," the guard said, nudging Alhud.

"Just one, sir?" Typically, a slave who asked a question of a guard got nothing more than a beating for an answer. But the guards all knew Alhud well, and as long as he toed the line well, he could get away with some things most slaves could not.

"Word is, the Master bought as him a favor to a rich friend," the guard said with a shrug. Knowing that was more than he could have hoped for in terms of information, Alhud simply nodded.

Soon, the new slave was brought to them. His hood was pulled off, and Alhud almost gasped in surprise. The newcomer was the palest man he had ever seen. Alhud had read enough about the world to know that the lands to the east were populated by a paler race of men. But he had never thought to see one here, a slave to the Noemi.

The man had blond hair and striking blue eyes. He was tall and well built. His clothes had once been nice, but hung about him in tatters. There was something about the way he stood, an almost casualness, as if he was not entering a life of servitude. He was soon loaded into the cart, his shackles attached to rings set on the side of the cart.

They were on their way back to the inner city of Noem when Alhud decided he might as well begin his work.

"What is your name, friend?" Alhud asked it gently; he wanted to establish a bond of comradery early. He had found that the newcomers listened and learned better under such treatment.

"I am no friend of yours, slaver." The man said it with no heat, just a simple statement of fact. Alhud allowed himself a small smile.

"I am actually a slave myself," Alhud began, "but you need not tell me your name. If you do not care to name yourself, one will be chosen for you."

"Terrin," the man responded.

"Good. Now Terrin, how did you come to be here? I confess I have never met one of the eastern peoples." Alhud gestured around to the city around them. "And if you have any questions for me, now is the time for asking." Terrin stared at him a long time before speaking.

"Are you trying to bond or something?" Terrin asked, his voice toneless. "Does it make it easier for you to order your own kind about if you pretend you are their friend?" Alhud was surprised that his tactic had been seen through so easily, although the rest of the question was entirely untrue.

"I think you misunderstand my position," Alhud said. "I am a simple slave, just like you. I was chosen to welcome you because I have been here for a long time. I have much knowledge that you will find helpful as you start your new life."

"I am not a slave," Terrin said, leaning forward as far as his bonds allowed. "I may be held here against my will, and I may be forced to labor for your masters, but I will never be a true slave. And someday, I will leave this place, return to my home, and destroy those who have caused me to be here." There was a little heat to his voice now, but his words were delivered as if he were telling Alhud that the sky was blue or that water was wet. He believed these things as incontrovertible fact.

"Guard," Alhud raised his voice slightly, "Could you take us to the outer city wall, west side of the city." The guard half turned his head so he could see Alhud out of the corner of his eye.

"Why would I do that?" The guard did not say it with the typical rancor that most guards would have when addressed by a slave. He was genuinely curious.

"I believe it will help the new slave to better understand his circumstances," Alhud said earnestly, "and that is what our master has tasked me with. So please, sir, take us to the outer wall."

"I don't ne—" Terrin began, but Alhud held up his hand, cutting him off.

"I think we can hold off on any more talk for now. You will understand my point soon enough." In truth, Alhud was concerned with how Terrin had been speaking, especially in earshot of the guard. The trip to the outer wall took some time, but they reached it a few hours before dawn.

When they arrived, Alhud led Terrin to the top of the wall, aware that the chafing of the shackles on Terrin's ankles must be terrible by now. When they reached the top, Alhud asked the guard to give them some space; he was a little surprised that the guard did not argue but allowed Alhud to lead Terrin a few hundred steps down the wall.

"Now, can you guess why I brought you here?" Alhud asked. Terrin shook his head.

"Look to the east, you will see the great sea you crossed to come here," Alhud began, "but look to the west, and you will notice an even greater sea. A sea of sand." Alhud gestured to the view beyond the wall, where the desert stretched on beyond sight. "If you were to escape this city, you would either have to swim at least several hundred miles before you found land, or else walk out into that," he indicated the desert again. "Either way, you die."

"So, you brought me up here to try to tame me?" Terrin asked. "Or to break my spirit? To show me the futility of my desire for freedom and convince me to bow meekly to the yoke?"

"Yes and no," Alhud answered. "Yes, because I believe that your desires are hopeless. No, because I admire your spirit. I have seen many new slaves with your strong will. Most break, and when they break, they become like animals. I would not see that happen to you or any other I could help."

"And the rest?" Terrin asked. "The ones who don't break?"

"They are buried out there." Alhud gestured again to the never-ending expanse of sand beyond the walls. "The other reason I brought you here, is that you were saying dangerous things in earshot of our guard. That is unwise." He shook his head slowly. "Word spreads quickly among the overseers. If they mark you as a troublemaker, things will go hard for you. Very hard." Terrin looked out over the sands thoughtfully.

"So," Alhud said, "tell me now. How did you come to be here?"

"You first," Terrin said. Alhud smiled at him and nodded. He told Terrin of his old life, how that had ended, and how he had found a tolerable existence in a mostly intolerable place. Terrin nodded and almost smiled at his story.

"That is well for you," Terrin said in a way that made Alhud believe he was sincere, "that you found a life for yourself here. But that will not work for me." He shook his head sadly. "No, there are people back where I come from who depend on me. I must escape." His voice grew harder. "As for how I came to be here? Murder. Betrayal. And all manner of ill luck." He turned himself to look at Alhud. His face was fierce and his eyes were like blue flame. "But I swear this, I will get back. I do not know how or when. But I will. Even if I have to tear apart this nest of vipers and burn it all the ground."

Alhud felt a shiver run down his spine. Terrin's words struck his mind like the ringing of a bell. He could not say why, but his mind turned to Arac's book. Terrin turned back to the desert, his voice softening. "But, for your sake, I will bide my time for now. I will bow and scrape, and I will make no trouble if I can avoid it."

"You have a strength to you," Alhud said, "and not only that which you carry in your muscles. I believe that you believe these things." Alhud shook his head. "But I think you are destined for a short life if you pursue this."

"Maybe," Terrin admitted, "but I do not think so, though I cannot give a reason as to why beyond my own stubbornness."

"You speak like an educated man," Alhud said. "What were you before you came here? Give me that one detail at least. For my own curiosity, before we return to our guard and I take you to the slave quarter." Terrin nodded slowly. He leaned in close, speaking softly.

"I was a prince."

Terrin turned and hobbled back toward where the guard waited. Alhud could not help but stand still, staring after him. His feet felt rooted to the spot, and his arms had broken out in gooseflesh. *A pale prince commanding a sea in storm.* Arac's words ran through Alhud's head. The answer to that strange man's vision seemed right in front of him. Two questions now arose. Did Alhud tell Obari or keep it to himself? And, which sea would the prince command? The sea of salt water? Or the sea of sand?

Awakening

The inside of the carriage was almost completely dark as it trundled down the old dirt road in the middle of the night. The Princess, Althea, dozed fitfully in one seat, her two handmaids sharing the bench opposite her. She had long black hair and a heart-shaped face. She was young, barely over twenty, but her was face was drawn with care and fatigue. The trip to the capital city of Carynth was taking longer than it should have. The royal carriage and its retinue of guardsmen had taken several detours, including this little-used road through the Pelreth Woods, in an effort toto keep their movements secret.

The Princess stirred as the carriage hit a particularly large bump in the road. She was displeased by the uncomfortable and lengthy journey; however, much she understood the necessity of it. Their mission had been one of incredible diplomatic importance. The recent unrest between the Jinnbinders and the masses had the potential tocould potentially upset the entire kingdom, if not the world.

For years now, the common typical attitude toward the Jinnbinders, those who bonded with spirits of the elements to gain power, had devolved almost to the point of open violence. Althea had never had a particular dislike of the Jinnbinders, nor had she any particular fondness for them. She understood their importance in many industries and institutions, but their power also gave them unparalleled advantages when compared to people who could not commune with the elemental spirits.

Tales of Jinnbinders disappearing had begun to run rampant throughout the kingdom of Florys. Some claimed that they were being hunted; others said they were gathering in secret places, trying to mass their strength in order to take control of the land, and, eventually, all of Eoam. Althea was not sureunsure which version was true, but her journey to the small village of Toris, as well as others, had confirmed at least that the Jinnbinders were vanishing. There had been four Jinnbinders living in Toris, and within a single day, all four had disappeared. No one had any indication where they had gone or why.

Althea was ruminating on the possibilities that she and her advisors had discussed when the first scream split the air. It was the sound of a horse that had suffered a grievous wound. Her first thought was that one of the guardsmen's mounts had thrown a shoe or broken a leg on the uneven path. But that notion was quickly undercut by the call to arms of the other guardsmen. Shouts of panic and screams of pain filled the night air around the carriage. Althea was about to open the window of the carriagecarriage window to ask what was happening when the first thud hit the wall beside her. A second thud followed, this one harder, and the head of a crossbow bolt appeared beneath the window, inches from piercing her arm.

The two handmaids screamed at the sight of the barbed head protruding through the wood. Althea grabbed the younger of the two, a thin blonde girl named Tabby, and pulled her toward the carriage door on the opposite side of where the crossbow struck.

"Come," Althea said, firmly. "We must flee. We can try to find shelter in the woods until the guards have fought off the attack." She said it with a confidence she did not truly genuinely feel, but she could think of nothing else to do, and she refused to simply sit in the carriage and wait to die. She opened the door and pulled Tabby out. The other handmaid, a heavy older woman named Betha, followed quickly.

Outside the carriage was chaos. Horses screamed and men shouted. Steel rang against steel and arrows flew through the darkness. Torches held by some of the guards lit small pockets of violence in the night. The smell of blood was in the air.

"This way," Althea said, still pulling Tabby along. "We need to get to the cover of the trees." They hurried through the darkness toward the tree line at the edge of the road. It was difficult challenging to move quickly over the rough ground in the dark. Just as Althea reached the woods, with Tabby right behind her, she heard a gasping sound from several paces back.

Althea turned and saw Betha swaying by the edge of the road, torchlight playing on the bloody, barbed head of the crossbow bolt sticking out of her chest. Betha collapsed after a moment;, her body splayed at an odd angle on the ground. Althea felt tears sting her eyes, knowing they could not go back, and even if they could, there was nothing to be done. Betha was dead.

"Come on," Althea urged quietly to Tabby, who was staring wide-eyed in horror at the body. "We need to keep moving." They turned back and moved further into the woods.

"Into the trees! They're getting away!"

The shouts rang out of the darkness behind them, alerting Althea to two things. The first was that their escape had been noticed. The second, and more alarming, was that they were clearly wanted alive. Or rather, Althea herself was wanted. There were vVery few enemies of her family's house who would dare to make such a move as abducting the Princess so close to the capital. But, now was not the time to dwell on who it might be; now was the time to run.

"Hurry, now! We have to run!" Althea said to Tabby. They began moving more quickly into the woods, Althea still pulling Tabby along by the hand. It was difficult tTrying to run through the tangled, muddy undergrowth was difficult, especially in their long dresses. The terrain quickly changed from level to uphill, making their progress even slower. If Althea had

had some training in woodcraft, she might have tried to evade their pursuers in the dark, but she doubted that she would be able to hide herself and Tabby for very long with no such skills. Her only hopes were in getting far enough away and hoping the guards would overcome their attackers and follow to find the Princess and her maid.

The sounds of their pursuit were all around them in the night. Shouts filled the air of the woods, as well as the sound of heavy bodies crashing through the bushes. Althea soon realized that they had no chance to outrun the men chasing them, and instead dragged Tabby down into the hollow of a massive elm's large roots. They huddled together in the darkness, listening to the sounds of pursuit get ahead of them.

After a time, the sounds faded, and Althea decided to risk turning back toward the road. Hopefully, the pursuers were far enough ahead to not realize where they had lost their prey, and by now, the guards should have won the fight by the road. It took far longer to get back than it had to get to where they had hidden. It was almost dawn when they reached the road. They came out of the woods several hundred feet behind where they had fled, but they could still see the carriage on the road.

It was exactly where they had left it, although it had been thoroughly ransacked when Althea and Tabby reached it. The rest of the scene was not at all what she had been expecting. The road was a mess of dead men and horses. Blood had soaked the ground, leaving a brownish-red mess of mud. There had been were two score guards when before the attack, and almost twice that number lay dead in the road. As far as Althea could tell, each and every one of her guards had been slain. They had taken their share of the ambushers with them, though that was little solace to the princess.

What Althea could see of the attackers told her little. They were men of all races, not just Floryans like herself. There were men of Kuth, Rhupar, and Chull, as well as men she could not identify by nationality. They all wore simply simple black garb, with chainmail over it. Black cloaks and black hoods as well. Their weapons were all similar; simple but well made. They bore no sigils or identifying marks that she could see.

Althea was about to suggest to Tabby that they move on, when she heard a gasp and a whimper from behind her. She turned to see a man, dressed like the dead attackers, holding Tabby by the hair; a long, cruel-looking knife held to her throat. Several more men were stepping out of the trees behind him.

"Easy now, m'lady." The man holding the knife said. He was a tall, well-built man with long dark hair and a thin face. A scar on his cheek pulled at the left side of his mouth, twisting his mouth into a leery, half-grin. "Give us no trouble, and this young lady'll be fine." A couple of the other men had come up behind Althea now, and she briefly considered making a break for the trees or putting up some sort of fight. But, seeing the knife at Tabby's throat, she knew she could not do it. She felt one of the men forced force her wrists together in front of her body, while the other bound them with a length of coarse rope. Tabby was quickly bound in a similar fashion.

"Go find the others," the scarred man said to one of the other men. "Tell them to meet us at the rendezvous. Then we can head back to the ship." The man he addressed loped off into the woods.

"Shouldn't we just take them to the ships now?" One of the remaining men offered, slowly. "Lord Isar will be waiting." The scarred man looked at him with a stern gaze.

"No," he said, firmly. "We will go when we're all together. I ain't leaving the rest of the men out here. What if someone gets caught? What if they talk? No, we meet up and go together." Althea was trying to process this information. Someone wanted her alive, but she had never heard of this "Lord Isar" before. He must be some catspaw for one of the other high nobles. It was the only explanation that made any sense.

With no further objections, the men prepared to leave the road. First, they lashed a rope between Althea's wrist bonds and Tabby's waist, then a second rope from Tabby's wrist, which one of the men held and used to pull them along.

The abductors began to lead the two captive women off the road on the opposite side from where they had fled during the attack. Like the other side, this one quickly turned uphill. There were no paths, so the progress was slow. Even with their captors tugging them along like recalcitrant cattle, they made bad terrible time. After several hours, their dresses were torn and muddy, they had been scratched and scraped by the close press of branches, and their feet were aching from walking in shoes that were barely more than slippers. They stopped to rest just twice as the day wore on and they were given no more than a hard crust of bread to eat. The land dipped and rose constantly, though it continued to trend uphill.

Finally, as dusk was beginningbegan to settle into full dark, they stopped again. The men began to prepare a camp for the night, when one of them noticed a light farther up the hill.

"Dageth!" one of the men whispered, urgently.. "Look! A fire! Maybe its it's some of the men." The scarred man, Dageth, looked up toward the light that was barely perceptiblebarely perceptible light through the trees.

"Nah," said Dageth, "probably just some hunters. All our men were on the other side of the road." He smiled at the man, a sickly, ugly sort of grin. "Perhaps they have food, and perhaps they'd be willing to *share*." He laughed at his own ugly joke, the other men joining in.

"Someone go see how many they are. Mayhaps we'll get some hot food tonight."

One of the men scurried of off quickly and quietly through the trees, like a seasoned woodsman. He returned after a few moments. "Just two of 'em, sir," he said with a sly grin. "And they got a bird on the fire." Althea felt her stomach clench at the thought of a warm meal, even though she knew no part of it would go to herself or Tabby. She also felt sick at the thought idea of the two men up the hill, two more murders to be added to these rogues' list.

Dageth led the rest of the men, save the one holding the prisoners' ropes, up the hill toward the fire. Althea and Tabby were dragged along at the rear.

The two men sitting around the fire were dressed as foresters. Both wore hunting leathers and large cloaks. One was in all browns and greens, with a brown cloak with the hood thrown back. He had brown hair tied into a knot behind his head, a thick brown beard, and green eyes that shone like emeralds in the firelight. He wore a sword at his hip, the scabbard sticking back and digging into the ground behind where he sat. The second man wore all black. The cowl of his black cloak hung low over his face, so very little of his face was visible beyond his bearded chin. He was short and stocky, with shoulders like and an ox. He wore a short sword over his back.

The two men had just pulled some sort of roasted bird off the spit hanging over the fire and split it apart between them when Dageth swaggered into the clearing, his men spreading out around him. Althea and Tabby were dragged into the open area last, and shoved to the ground by the man guarding them. . They showed no surprise at seeing these strangers, though the man in brown lowered his leg of meat to rest on one of the stones around the fire. The man in black dug into his leg without hesitation.

"Welcome," said the man in brown. "Are you looking to share our fire?" He showed no concern at for these armed men, although his eyes widened slightly when he noticed Althea and Tabby. "We don't have much food to share, but the fire is big enough to warm us all." Dageth seemed to notice their cavalier attitude, and the fact that they were armed, and held back at the edge of the clearing a bit. The other seven men spread out and advanced a few steps forward.

"Kind of you to offer," Dageth said, companionably, "but I think you've more to share than you're letting on. Plus, it's been a few days since we had a warm meal, and even one bird would go a long way." The threat was evident in his voice, but the two men around the fire still seemed unperturbed. The man in the brown cloak stood up slowly.

"It's a shame you feel that way," the man said. "As it happens, we might have enough for two more. Perhaps we could spare some for the two women you've brought with you." There was something dangerous about the man now, a sense of comfortable power about him. As if he challenged large groups of armed men frequently and saw no danger in it. The man in black simply continued to eat, tearing a strip of meat from the bone with the practiced ease of a man accustomed to eating meat from a fresh kill.

"I'm afraid the women ain't up to eating just now." Dageth returned evenly. "They've had their fill. But my men, well, they've had a busy day. And I don't know if they're willing to pass up a chance at fresh meat… however they have to get it." The man in brown frowned a little, the first show of any sort of emotion from either man.

"We don't take kindly to slavers or 'nappers around here." The man said it simply, but there waswith an edge of steel in his voice. His hand moved to rest on the hilt of his blade. "I think it'd be best if you left the ladies with us and went off in search of easier prey." Dageth's jaw clenched at this. Althea was surprised he hadn't simply attacked. Perhaps he was stalling, hoping more of their men would show up and add to their advantage.

"We're no slavers." Dageth's voice had some heat now. "These two are runaways and wanted by our master. And its it's not business of yours, nor do I see how you could stop us if it was. Now, unless you want a fight, clear out and leave all your gear. Or things could get ugly."

"Looking at you, I don't see how they could get uglier," the man in brown quipped. "Unfortunately, we'll have to decline your generous offer. Right, Tal?" He looked down at the man in black.

"Tal?" The man prodded again when the man in black ignored him in favor of his food.

"I'm eating." The hooded man replied simply. "Been too long since we had fresh fowl."

"Tal!" The man in brown sounded annoyed now. Dageth's men began to advance now, four to one side of the fire, two toward the other. Dageth held back, as did the man guarding the two women. Althea was completely utterly puzzled by the complete lack of concern shown by this "Tal". Even the man in brown seemed more annoyed with his fellow than with the advancing armed men.

"Tal!" the man repeated, actual irritation plain in his voice.

"Beron!" Tal replied in a high, mimicky mimicking voice. The man in brown, Beron, sighed before replying.

"Tal, please." This time the Tal sighed, tossing away the leg bone he had been gnawing at. He rose to his feet, stretching his arm up and behind his head, then holding the pose as if stretching.

"Fine," Tal said. "You want to do the killing or the freeing?" He asked this question as if it was an old pastime of theirs.

"The freeing, if you don't mind." ," Beron responded, as he bent down and touched the ground, muttering something inaudible. Then he drew his sword and sprang at the man circling around the fire closest to him. Tal's arms whipped forward, and two of the men closest to him fell, knives sprouted sprouting from their throats, blood fountaining into the air. He pulled two more knives blades from inside his cloak and threw them before the next two men could react. One fell with a knife in his eye, the; the other man toppled with a knife in his chest. In the blink of an eye, the odds had gone from six on two to two on two.

Beron was fighting one of the remaining two and was clearly the superior warrior. It did not take him long to disarm the man and bury his longsword in the man's stomach. He left the dying man behind and approached the one guarding the two women.

Tal had already drawn his short sword and dispatched the remaining man; he was now engaging with Dageth himself. As Beron fought the guard, Althea felt an odd sensation near her hands. She looked down and saw a creature of some kind gnawing at her bonds. The thing was like a shadow, but a shadow made of earth. It was similar to a squirrel but largerbigger with and it had large, bright green eyes. She yelped in shock and nearly fell backwards backward as she realized what it was.

It was an earth Jinn. One of these men was a Jinnbinder.

Althea remembered what Beron had done before the fight began, whispering to the earth. It was clearly him. The Jinn looked at her curiously and made a chittering sound.

"Don't be frightened, my lady." Althea looked up to see Beron standing over her. "He's only trying to help." She realized that her bonds were loose now. The Jinn had freed her. Beron pulled a knife from his belt and bent down to cut Tabby's bonds as well.

"There are more of these men in the woods," Althea warned Beron, trying to get over her fright. There was something other than fright there though. A feeling in her bones that felt like something familiar. Beron nodded at her warning as he sawed through Tabby's bonds.

Dageth and Tal were fighting all across the clearing now. It was clear that Dageth was an expert swordsman, though for some reason, it seemed that Tal was holding him off without trying very hard. Almost as if he was toying with Dageth. Althea tried to pay attention to the fight, but that feeling inside her was growing. She could not tell what it was, but the fire on the other side of the clearing seemed to be catchingcatch her eye more than was natural. It was almost hypnotizing.

"Tal!" Beron called. "We need to get away. There are more of them around here somewhere." Tal only grunted in response. Tabby was free now and she was allowingallowed Beron to help rub some life back into her hands.

"Tal! End it!" Beron shouted again. Maybe Tal really was toying with Dageth.

"Don't tell me my business!" Tal snapped back.

Suddenly, a shape moved up behind Beron. It was the guard; he must not have been killed by Beron in their fight. The silver of his knife glinted in the firelight.

The firelight drew Althea's attention again, even in that dire moment. It… it seemed to call to her. Knowing she had to act fast or Beron would be killed, she acted on instinct and answered the call from somewhere inside herself.

It wasn't an audible word or a distinct command. But suddenly, a shape flew from the fire and struck the guard in the head. In fact, it did not simply strike his head, it; it engulfed it in flame. He fell to the ground screaming.

Beron rolled away from the man, staring at him in surprise. Then he turned to look at Althea, as a shape made of pure fire left the man on the ground, and flew toward her. A bird made of pure flame circled her head a few timesIt circled her head a few times, a bird made of pure flame. By instinct, she held out her wrist like a falconer receiving their raptor, and the fiery bird alit on the offered perch. She felt no heat from the creature except for a comforting warmth.

"Bregna's Tits!" Beron swore. "You're a Jinnbinder!" Althea could not believe it herself. But it was impossible to deny that this creature was a Jinn, like the one Beron had summoned.

"H-h-how do I tell it to go?" Althea asked, nervously. Beron seemed disappointed by the question.

"Just like you summoned it," Beron said simply. "Use that same feeling, and just tell it you no longer need its help." Althea closed her eyes and felt around inside herself. She found that same feeling, and she pushed the dismissal through the link that she felt between herself and the flaming bird on her wrist. It gave a faint squawk and vanished in a puff of smoke.

"We really should be going," Althea said, shakily. She was trying to maintain her composure, but it was difficult. Beron nodded.

"Tal!" Beron called again, this time with real annoyance in his voice. "We need to go!"

"Fine!" Tal shouted back. The fight with Dageth had already been going poorly for the scarred man; he was bleeding from several small minor wounds. But something changed in Tal's movements. He moved more fluidly, and after a flurry of strokes, sent Dageth's sword flying. Dageth dove after, but Tal made no move to pursue him. Instead, Tal dropped his short sword, and held his empty hand out to the side. Smoke or shadow of some kind seem seemed to coalesce around his hand, until a black sword had formed there. The blade was made of some metal Althea had never seen. It seemed to drink light, the edges of it blurring against the firelight.

Dageth staggered to his feet, sword back in his hand. He eyed the strange sword uneasily, but threw himself back into the fight with determination. For a second, it seemed like he might take Tal by surprise. But at the last moment, Tal slid aside as easily as if he was dodging the flailings of a toddler. Tal brought the black blade up in an arc and cut through Dageth's sword as if the steel was nonexistent. The blow followed through, shearing through Dageth's neck like a hot knife through a soft cheese. The scarred man's head hit the ground with a soft thump.

Tal immediately released the sword, which disappeared into shadow. Althea had so many questions about what she had just seen, but she had no time to ask them. Beron took her warning to heart and began to pack up the camp quickly. Althea checked on Tabby to be sure she was ok. Tabby assured her she was, although she looked at her with a strange mixture of fear and fascination. Althea could understand. Jinnbinders were fearsome folk, and now, apparently, she was one of them.

Beron handed a piece of the bird they had roasted to Althea and Tabby, but told them they would need to eat as they walked. Althea had explained who she was while Beron was packing and he had said that he would escort her to somewhere safe where she could then make her way to Carynth.

"Take them to the river, Beron," Tal said, when they were ready to leave. "I'll make sure you're not followed." Althea was stunned by that, and tried to protest that there were many men out there who would be searching for her. Tal simply shrugged at her warnings and disappeared through the trees back the way Dageth had led them from.

"He'll be alrightall right," Beron said. "If there are too many, he'll simply hide. However, I doubt that there will be too many for him."

They began to walk down the far side of the hill. Beron explained as they walked how he would take her to the river Aelwed. From there, they could take a river barge to Carynth. Althea asked him questions about Jinnbinding and where the Jinnbinders had been disappearing too. He explained that the Jinnbinders had been gathering together to form their own community.

Beron told her of a warning he had received a year before, saying that it would soon become dangerous for the Jinnbinders to exist in peace anywhere in Eoam. When Althea pressed him for more information, all he would say was that the information came from a strange man. He was an old man, very short, with white hair and a white beard. He had told Beron things he could not possibly have known and had left after delivering his warning.

"As to teaching you," Beron said, hesitantly. "I'm afraid I can't do that. Not unless you decide to live with us." He seemed genuinely sad about it. "You'll need to find your own teacher, preferably one who has partnered with a fire Jinn, like you." Althea was not happy with that response, but no prodding or begging would change his mind.

Finally, around noon the following day, the they reached the river. It took about an hour of walking along the river to reach the outskirts of the trading town. Beron stopped them there and told them they would be safe enough without him now.

"There must be something I can do or give you to thank you for your help," Althea said. Beron shook his head but smiled as he did.

"No, my lady," Beron replied. "I could not accept any kind of payment. We were saving our own hides as much as yours." He smiled again. "However, I would ask that you keep in mind that most Jinnbinders are like myself. We don't abuse our powers and we want simplysimply want to live our lives. Remember that we are your subjects too, and we deserve protection, should it come to that."

"I will do what I can for your people." ," Althea promised.

"Ah, don't you mean *our* people?" Beron grinned again. "You've had your awakening. You are one of us too. Even if you never do more with it than you have."

With that, Beron turned and strode back into the woods. Althea turned back to Tabby, took her by the arm, and the two of them walked toward the town. She considered all that Beron had told her and decided that she would have to find herself a teacher.

The Cost of Vengeance

I held hard to the piece of driftwood as the waves tossed me back and forth. Saltwater sloshed in my mouth as I struggled to keep my head up, gasping in air whenever I could. After hours in the water, as the sun was starting to rise, I glimpsed land. It was a small spit of an island with a small, thick stand of trees looming beyond the beach. I paddled as hard as possible, and eventually, the tide took me, throwing me toward the beach, pulling me back slightly, then throwing me forward again.

As I struggled through the shallows and up onto the beach, I finally let go of the piece of wood that had saved my life. There was more wreckage on the beach, whether from our ship or the other one, I could not tell. The morning sun was beginning to beat down on the beach in force; sweat was beginning to drip from my skin, mixing with the salty seawater that covered me.

The beach extended several hundred feet in either direction before it began to curve. I guessed the island was small enough that I could walk around it in an hour or less. The trees loomed far above the high tide mark on the sand, a thick forest of tightly packed mangroves. I turned back to study the beach, hoping to find something useful in the wreckage when I noticed the man. He was sitting slumped against a large tree to my right. His head was tilted forward toward his chest as if he slept. I approached him warily, unsure if he was one of my crew or that of the ship we had been pursuing.

As I got closer, I could see more details of the man. His dark hair hung in a tangle around his face, though I could see a small, pointed beard adorned his chin. His soiled clothing must have been nice before the wreck. His hands were on his left thigh, where a thick makeshift bandage had been wrapped around some kind of wound. Despite the wrapping, there was blood on the sand beside him.

He looked up as I got closer, a quick jerk of the head that told me if he had not been unconscious before, he had been close to it. His hands tightened on the cloth around his leg as if he was preparing to rise quickly. I lifted my hands, palms out, to show him I meant no harm. He relaxed a bit, although the suspicion remained in his small, bright eyes.

"Ho, friend," I said softly, my voice rasping in my throat. "I have no wish to harm you. It looks like the two of us are the only survivors of the storm. What is your name?" He continued to eye me warily for a moment before he responded.

"I-I am ca—" he hacked a cough before starting again. "I am called Dirk." He coughed again, trying to clear his dry throat.

"Well, Dirk, I am Evin. I take it you were a member of Torkal's crew? I don't remember you from my ship."

He nodded weakly, grimacing as he shifted his injured leg.

"I was. Not by choice, really. Just needed the work." Dirk shook his head as if ashamed of his employment. I could understand that. I had done many things I did not enjoy in my life simply out of necessity.

"I can respect a man doing what he must. But now, we must arrange some sort of camp if we are to survive until some kind of rescue can come." It was unlikely such a rescue would come any time soon. We were far off the known trade routes when the storm hit, and it could have swept us further in the night. Dirk nodded his head in agreement and tried to rise.

"Woah," I said quickly. "Not so fast. It would not do for you to bleed out and leave me alone." I forced a chuckle and helped him to sit back down. I bid him wait and went to the edge of the tree line. I found a limb suitable for a crutch or at least a walking stick and broke it off as cleanly as I could with no blade. I stripped the smaller branches, leaving a Y-shape at the top.

With the stick under one arm, he was able to hobble down the beach toward where most of the wreckage lay. I helped him to sit on a slab of broken wood, and then began gathering up anything that might be useful. There were several chests and bags that had managed to find the shore; these I brought over to Dirk for him to sift through. With luck, there would be something to eat and drink in one of them.

It was past noon by the time I had scoured the wreckage. The sun was beating down fiercely. Dirk was sweating even more than I was and seemed about to pass out. I convinced him to lay back and draped a piece of sailcloth over a pair of sticks to create a sort of awning to protect him from the sun. His leg had bled more, but when I offered to look at it for him, he declined, saying he had done all that could be done for it. I told him to rest and that I would check out the forest and see if I could find something to eat or at least gather wood for a fire once the sun had gone down.

The forest quickly proved too thick to offer much more than some wood for the fire. The undergrowth was tough and clingy, grasping at my boots and tearing at my pants as I fought through it. The tightly packed trees with their low-hanging branches obstructed my view and battered at my face. Ivy clung to my arms and hands as I tried to push it aside. Ten men with machetes would have had difficulty making their way through this mess. I soon gave up after collecting a few armfuls of wood.

I could hear birds in the trees, but I never caught even a glimpse of one. Even if I did see them, I had no bow or arrow to try to take one for food. On top of that, I had never pulled a bow in my life, nor hunted for food in the wild. I was a city boy, and beyond knowing the basics of making a fire, I was completely out of my element here.

I returned to where I had left Dirk, surprised to find him sitting up and rifling through the things I had salvaged. I saw that he had organized much of what had been in the chests and bags. There were some salted foodstuffs, a couple of skins of water, and various items of clothing that were more or less ruined by now. As I sat across from him, I noticed he had used a new piece of cloth to wrap his wound.

I was exhausted from my short foray in the woods; sweat dripped from me more heavily than I could remember at any point in my life. Dirk could see how tired I was and wordlessly began to parcel out a meal for us. We ate a small, unsatisfying meal, and took a few swallows of water. It was not much, but it was better than before. The sun was beginning to sink toward the horizon, and I could think of nothing else that I could do.

I asked Dirk several questions about himself as I built a small stack of wood to light when the sun finally went down. By the time I was done arranging the wood, I could tell that Dirk was not interested in sharing his story, which was fine by me because I was itching to tell mine.

"Would you like to know how I got here?" I asked Dirk, sitting back against another piece of wreckage. He shrugged and said nothing else. His demeanor had become more relaxed, but I could still sense his wariness.

"Very well, then," I said. And so, I began to tell my unenthusiastic audience my story.

I was born in the rich port city of Benit in northern Karilos. My father was a wealthy merchant trader who owned several shipping galleys. It was a good time to be a merchant, what with the civil war in Kendar. The first five years of my life were lived in wealth and privilege. I had nannies and tutors and anything I wished; my father gave me. My mother doted on me. Life was good.

But things changed one summer. A wealthy young man had begun to visit my parents. He was around twenty years old, handsome, with dark curly hair and bright eyes. He had a prominent hawk-like nose and a strong jaw with a small scar across his chin. Under his influence, my parents began to throw lavish parties. They began to gamble and won a lot…at first. I do not know the young man's name; he called himself Paris, but I doubt that was his real name. He began to give my father business advice and to call on my mother when my father was away. I did not understand the implications of these visits; I only knew that my mother no longer seemed to have time for me.

It all ended when I heard my parents arguing one night. They screamed at each other, each blaming the other for whatever problems had arisen. I learned later that Paris had disappeared, with a sizeable sum of my parents' wealth. He had also convinced my father to take out loans to increase his business. Loans that my father could no longer keep up with. I still remember the day I found my father in the orchard behind our house. He was hanging from one of the taller trees, his face bloated and discolored.

Things changed quickly after that. My mother and I were forced to move out of our nice house and into a small apartment by the docks. All my father's assets were sold to cover his debts, and we were left with very little. I was almost seven when my mother took sick. It was some wasting illness of the body, but I could see in her eyes that her soul was sick as well. Her will to live had died with my father, and now her body was following suit.

On her deathbed, she pulled me close and spoke to me with more force than she had in a long time.

"Grow strong, Evin," she told me. "Grow up strong. It will be hard, but you must grow strong."

Her fingers curled around my upper arm and pulled me closer. Her eyes were hard and bright; there was more life in her here at the end than there had been in months.

"And when you are strong enough," she continued, "find that bastard. Find him and kill him. Kill him slow. Make him suffer for ruining our lives."

Those were the last words my mother ever spoke to me. After her death, I was sent to an orphanage. I spent six years learning how to avoid bullies and take care of myself. My only drive was to fulfill my mother's dying wish. However, I had no idea how to do that.

One night, I went to an inn called the Spar. It was an inn known for a particular storyteller beloved by all the locals. I had heard of this man and wanted to hear what his stories were like. I had not listened to a good story since before Paris came into my life.

The storyteller was just about to begin when I entered. I stood at the back and watched him avidly. He was a short man. Older, with long white hair and a long white beard. His eyes were bright blue, and his brows were sharply peaked at the corners. He was stick-thin, but he did not seem frail at all.

"So," he began, rubbing his hands together as if warming them. "Tonight, I will tell the tale of Sir Talon, the Tragic. It is a seldom told tale, but an important one, I think." As he spoke, I became enraptured. It was like he was speaking just for me. In fact, it seemed at times that he was looking directly at me.

"Sir Talon was a mighty knight of old Kendar, before the civil war, when the land was one," he said. "But Talon had his flaws as well. He was headstrong and oblivious to reason at times. When he had a problem, he clung to it like a dog to a bone until he solved it. This passion served him well in many ways, but it was also his downfall." The storyteller went on to tell of how Talon fell in love with a beautiful woman. They married and had children; their life was good. Until one day, a band of pirates attacked his town and murdered his family. Talon vowed to find the pirates and slay them. He traveled all over the world, searching for the murderers. He begged help from kings, his fellow knights, and even commoners. But, none of them could offer him any aid of substance.

"At last, he became so desperate he sought out the fabled Runewardens. An ancient order of magicians that were said to be almost all-powerful." The storyteller looked around at the audience, seeing *their horror at his invoking of this near-forbidden legend. "He found one after many years of searching, and begged his help. The Runewarden asked him what cost would he be willing to pay for his vengeance. 'Anything! Any cost at all!' Talon replied. Twice more the Runewarden asked, and twice more Talon responded. 'Anything! Any cost at all!' And so, the Runewarden took three drops of Talon's blood and chanted a mighty spell. The Runewarden gave Talon an amulet made from the drops of his blood and told him it would help him find the men he sought."*

The storyteller's eyes were now locked on mine, and I could feel the power of his gaze. Some part of me knew this story was meant for me.

"Talon traveled with the amulet leading him," the old man continued, "and he found the pirates who had slaughtered his family. He slew them all, but as the last one fell dead, so too did Talon. As he lay dying, his own words rang in his ears. 'Anything! Any cost at all!' His life was the cost, and the cost was paid. And so ended Sir Talon the Tragic."

The story struck me hard, but not in the way in which the storyteller intended, if indeed he had meant the story for me. Instead of warning me of the hazards of vengeance, it gave me the idea that to get what I desired, I needed to find a Runewarden.

Several more years passed. The fires of my hatred for Paris dulled as I grew up. I was soon too old for the orphanage and found myself on the streets. At sixteen, I joined an abbey. Not out of any desire for religious pursuit, it was simply my only option for survival. I learned about the gods; the Skymother, the Tidefather, and the Earthgrinder. I learned all about their legends and their mighty powers. But they were never more than stories for me. I was quickly deemed unfit for life as a priest, but the abbot gave me a job cleaning the abbey instead.

I had all but given up on vengeance or anything other than a life of menial servitude when I overheard a man during his confession. He was speaking to one of the priests of man he had worked for. He had thought the man was a merchant, but after setting sail, he realized the man was a pirate, preying on other merchants. The man he described matched my recollection of Paris perfectly, even down to the scar on his chin. He called the man Captain Torkal and said he had been preying on ships for over two years now.

Overhearing this conversation reignited the coals of my desire for revenge. I quit the abbey that day and went down to the docks. I spent the next few days attempting to get hired on a merchant ship. Unfortunately, I had no experience on ships. I knew nothing of how they functioned and no one was willing to take me on to learn.

After almost a week of no success, I drowned my misery in a drafty little inn, which I don't recall the name of. I was quite drunk when a man sat down beside me. He was of average height and wiry. His hair and beard were grey and all the same length, like an iron frame made for his face. He had heavy brows the same shade, and eyes so dark it looked almost as if they had no pupil.

He inquired about my business in the inn, and in my inebriated state, I told him far more than I would have normally. I told him of my quest for vengeance and my inability to get hired on a ship.

"I might be able to help you out there," he said stroking his chin, "I have a friend who is looking for deckhands. He might be willing to take you on and teach you if I asked him to."

"And why would you do that for me?" His sudden and generous offer had shaken a little of my stupor off, but I was still suspicious. The man shrugged before responding.

"I like to do people favors," he said, "providing they agree that someday they'd be willing to repay it." He smiled in a way that was just short or predatory. But, in my drunken state and my

excitement at the prospect of getting hired, I ignored it. After all, what was one favor against the realization of my life's mission for vengeance? I agreed quickly. I asked his name as he was rising to leave.

"I've gone by many names over the years," he said with a smile, "but you can call me Isar."

The next day I went down to the docks and presented myself at a merchant ship called the Golden Erne. I spoke with the captain, a man named Orsen. He agreed to take me on as Isar had said, and then he sent me to a man named Remir to begin my training.

For the better part of three years, I learned everything there was to know about sailing. I learned to tie a hundred different knots, how to climb the rigging, and reef the sails. I learned how to fight, both honorably and otherwise. I learned to keep a knife concealed in my sleeve, held in place by a cleverly knotted thong that would release when I flexed my forearm in a certain way. I became especially talented at taking the gods' names in vain. In that time, I had become one of Orson's most trusted men, second only to Remir himself.

Finally, I believed the time was right to broach the subject of my true goals with the captain. I did it subtly, first bringing up the rumors of a great pirate who had amassed an incredible fortune. I painted a picture of how much that pirate must have taken by now. I planted the idea that if we could capture this pirate, that fortune could be ours. I never told him about my true mission. I let him think I was simply greedy. But, being a greedy man himself, he began to come around. Pretty soon, I had him convinced that we could do it. We hired a troop of armed guards and traveled south toward the islands that Torkal was known to prowl.

We spent months sailing through the maze of islands that clogged that area of the sea. More than once, Orsen became impatient and wished to give up the chase. But each time, I was able to lure him back with thoughts of the vast fortune we would get for taking down Torkal.

At last, we caught our first sight of Torkal's ship, the Dancing Crane. We were pulling into port on an island called Carith, when we saw her putting out to sea so close to us, we could have thrown a line onto her. We pulled the Erne around and set off after Torkal's ship. The Crane was a swift ship, far faster than most merchant galleys. But the Erne was not most merchant galleys. She was a swift ship with an experienced crew who knew her well.

Our pursuit lasted for days. We chased them through narrow straits and across the open, endless sea. Our supplies were low, as we had not docked at Carith's harbor, and the Crane's holds were likely full to bursting. That likely made all the difference in our pursuit, and day by day, we began to creep closer.

But as the gap between us began to narrow, the weather began to worsen. The winds blew harsh, yet fickle. First this way, then that. Our rations were running low, but our resolve was unbent. I was a force myself, running hither and thither across the deck, helping where I could and screaming encouragement where I could not.

At last, in an open area of the sea that was familiar to none of us, the gap was at its closest. Unfortunately, the weather was at its worst. As we gained more and more on our prey, a massive storm began to form behind us. We put out all the oars and hung out all the sail we could. We needed to catch the Crane before this massive storm hit us. The wind aided both ships equally, but we had the advantage in oars and the gap continued to shrink.

Just when it seemed we would win out, the storm hit. The winds howled around us, and the thunderheads turned day into night. Rain lashed the deck, and lightning lit the sky with terrible frequency. I was at the wheel for the worst of it, guiding our way through what felt like a night in Hell. Remir had taken charge of the deck, bellowing his orders to the hands, while Captain Orsen stood at my shoulder. He was resolute at first, but as the storm worsened, he grew ever more fretful. Twice he offered that we should give up and try to turn out of the storm's path. I ignored him both times. As the ship pitched to and from, his suggestions became orders. On any ship, a captain's orders are law, but I ignored them just the same.

Finally, Orsen became fed up with my insolence and tried to wrest the wheel from me. We strove back and forth, him screaming his orders to give in, me silently trying to maintain course. At last, a massive wave washed over the aft deck. Orsen was washed to the rail, and I was thrown to the deck near him. As he stood shakily, clutching the rail, I saw my chance. One question remained in my mind. What cost was I willing to pay for my vengeance? Any cost. Anything at all.

With that resolution in mind, I threw myself at the captain. We grappled for a few precious seconds before I managed to heave him over the side. Not giving myself time to contemplate my sin, I dove back for the wheel and righted our course. The Crane had pulled away again in the interim, but I refused to quit.

As the gale continued to worsen around us, I drove the ship forward unrelentingly.

Remir found me at the wheel, screaming questions about the captain over the howling wind. I screamed back that he had been swept overboard. Remir ran to the side, as if the captain might be bobbing in the waves right below. He turned to me then and ordered me to turn back. He was about to try to take the wheel from me, but I had anticipated his actions. As he reached for the wheel, I went for my knife. I plunged it into his stomach as his hand reached the wheel. He fell to the deck and crawled toward the steps down to the deck. I let him go.

We were less than a hundred yards behind the Crane now, though I could barely see it in the darkness of the raging storm. But it did not matter to me. I was in charge of the ship now, and I would never give in. On and on we went, plunging up and over massive wave after massive wave. The storm pitched us side to side, but I drove us on.

Suddenly, I felt a hand on my arm. I looked to the side and saw Isar standing beside me. I could not fathom how he came to be there. He was not one of our crew.

"You must stop!" Isar bellowed over the winds. "You owe me a favor and I am calling it in!

Stop now and pull out of this storm!" His eyes were hard and I almost quailed before his stern gaze. Something in those eyes terrified me. But I still had my knife, and before he could say more, I swung it at his head. He pulled back far enough to avoid the worst of it, but I still felt the steel bite flesh. He fell from my sight, tumbling back toward the stairs and down to the deck.

Now I was truly gone. I had left all reason behind as we crept closer and closer to the Crane. A fey moon was on me, and I began to laugh a maniacal, insane sort of laugh. All these obstacles to my goal, and here I was, minutes from reaching it. I screamed commands to the men below, though I doubt they heard me. I bellowed curses at the Skymother and the Tidefather. I taunted them, degrading them for daring to stand in my way. I howled my wild exhortations to the sea below and the stars above, to thwart me if they could. I was unstoppable.

And then, the mast snapped.

A great, grinding sound like a massive whetstone on the blade of the earth rend the air. The main mast tipped and plunged into the sea. Thunder crashed as lightning tore the air at a frequency that could only be described as otherworldly. More grinding and shattering noises followed. And then, the deck exploded beneath my feet, and darkness enveloped me.

"And next I knew, I was clinging to driftwood, heading toward this island," I finished, gazing at Dirk. The firelight played across his hawk-like nose and sunken cheeks. It highlighted his strong jaw, all except the small pointed beard on his chin, that I was certain concealed a scar.

"Now you know how I came to be here…. Paris." I said it simply, for I had known this whole time who he was. His face was etched indelibly in my mind, and even near twenty years of aging could not disguise him from me. "Or Torkal, if you prefer. I'm sure neither are your true name."

The shock registering on his face was almost priceless. He clutched his wounded leg and made as if to try to stand, but stayed huddled against the wreckage at his back. I had had enough time during our day together to observe him and determine he was unarmed. That, and the fact he was injured would make him an easy target. Plus, I still had my knife hidden in my sleeve.

"I vowed to pay any cost, anything at all." I said, "anything just to find you and have my revenge." I considered this man before me. This poor, beaten creature. It would be simple to kill him, even to torture him, as my mother had asked. I also considered the story of Sir Talon. And I came to a decision.

"And I have decided that my cost," I said, staring him in the eye, "is forgiveness." I let him digest my words as I stood up and opened my arms. "I have decided that the cost of my vengeance, is the vengeance itself. I choose not to follow Talon's path and to forgive you instead." Torkal eyed me suspiciously, but slowly levered himself to his feet, his hands still clutching the wrappings to his injured leg.

I walked forward and embraced him. My arms went around his lean form, one hand grasping his shoulders…but the other hand I held to the side and flexed my forearm. The knife slid from my sleeve, the hilt finding my palm with practiced ease.

As I plunged my knife into his back, sliding it between the ribs to strike his heart, I saw a flash of silver and grunted as he pulled his own knife and drove it into my chest. I realized too late why he had clutched those bandages so tight. He had been hiding a knife there from the beginning.

Torkal's body fell backward, boneless, but I managed to take a few stumbling steps before collapsing facedown in the sand. He had just missed my heart; still a fatal blow, but not as quick as the one I had dealt him. I could see his body from the corner of my eye — his limp form darkening the sand with his life's blood. My breathing became shallow, and blood dribbled from my lips.

A shape moved at the edge of my vision. A figure materializing itself into the form of a man. A man I recognized.

Isar.

He walked up to the lifeless body of Torkal, tipping the dead man's head to the side with the toe of his boot.

"Hmmm, what a waste," Isar said, "he has been so useful over these past years." He turned and looked at me. There was no breath in my lungs to speak, I could only listen.

"You could have been useful too," he said sadly. "If only you had listened to me, you could have served a higher purpose. Ah, well. There have been others before you, and there shall be more after." With that, he turned and strode back into the trees.

I had no idea where he had come from or where he was going. But I was certain now that he was no mere man. And that our meeting at that bar had been no accident. Not that it mattered now. Not with so little time left to me.

I considered my life. More than twenty years of living, and most of it spent in pursuit of revenge. Only to end up here, bleeding out in the sand of some nameless island far from home. I considered the vow I had made; the same vow Sir Talon had made. Any cost, anything at all. After all this, all I could think to myself was one thing.

Worth it.

The Ten Towers of Tarah

The moon rose high in the sky over the shining, silver city of Tarah as Elodan ran through the smooth-paved streets. He was eager to reach his destination; he could even see it now, the Tower of Vinaya, rising high above the well-ordered buildings. Tonight was a special night, the Festival of the Spring Dawn. Tonight, all across the city, the Druadan would be taking to the rooftops and high places of the city to celebrate through the night and welcome the first rising sun of the new spring.

This was the first such festival that Elodan, just ten years old, had been permitted by his parents to attend for the entire night. Not only that, but his tutor, Master Talorin, had invited all his students to take in the sights of the celebration from the Tower itself. It was a tremendous honor and privilege to be allowed inside one of the Towers, let alone to go all the way to the top for a whole night.

Elodan turned down a final street and skidded to a stop before the grand staircase leading up the doors of the Tower. Talorin was already waiting atop the steps, his arms folded in the sleeves of his voluminous robes, his piercing green eyes and long white hair visible in the shining moonlight that seemed to reflect throughout the city. Elodan could see he was the last to arrive, his fellow students Jarin and Dorilla both waiting behind their master. Jarin, a year older than Elodan, waited patiently while Dorilla seemed barely able to contain her enthusiasm, her beaming smile stretching across her face from ear to ear.

"Nice of you to join us, Elodan," Talorin said softly. He was not a harsh master, but he was a stickler for punctuality. Elodan felt flush under the light criticism. He was not technically late, but the sounds of revelry from nearby rooftops made it clear that the celebration was well underway. Talorin turned to look at his other charges as Elodan joined them near the door. "I believe we are ready to proceed," he began as he produced a long silver key from his sleeve. "I know I have already warned you three, but I feel I must repeat myself. While we are within the Tower proper, it is important to remain silent and respectful. This is a holy place."

The three youngsters nodded their heads in near unison. Talorin gave them a last considering look before inserting the key into the lock of the large, silver door of the Tower. They entered one by one and found themselves in a large circular chamber with a towering statue of Vinaya, the Goddess of the Moon and Stars herself. The figure was imposing and welcoming all at once. A staircase wound around the Tower's inner walls, spiraling up in a seemingly endless circle towards the top. Everything in the Tower shone with the moon's silvery light, though there was no apparent source for it.

Talorin led the small group to the staircase and began to ascend the seemingly endless spiral of steps. The steps grew straight out from the wall of the Tower and had no railing to bar the edges, despite the stairs not being wide enough for more than a single person to use at once. Elodan soon grew weary of the monotonous steps; his legs and feet ached from climbing step after step, winding around and around the inside of the Tower. He looked up to see how much further it would be, but he still could see no end to their journey.

Elodan then made the mistake of looking down. He had not realized, despite his weariness of the ascent, how far above the entrance hall they had climbed. The statue of Vinaya was still visible, but it seemed such a small thing from such a height. His head began to swim as thoughts of what it would be like to fall from this high up. His knees shook as he thought about the feeling of his bones breaking and his body shattering from the fall. He tried to turn his mind from these things, but he could not. He tried to turn his eyes from the stones far beneath himself, but he could not.

Suddenly, a hand gripped Elodan's shoulder. A warm, calming feeling flooded his body. He looked up at Talorin. The older man smiled at him.

"It's ok," Talorin said reassuringly. "Some people don't handle the heights well. Just keep your eyes ahead and don't think about the drop." That seemed easier said than done to Elodan, but once Talorin turned to resume his ascent, Elodan did find it easier to ignore the dark thoughts, and he did not look down again as they climbed toward the tower top.

At last, they reached the landing at the top of the winding staircase. Talorin produced a key from within his robes and unlocked the door there with it. The foursome emerged onto the top of the Tower to the incredible sight of the city in full swing of the festival.

Elodan had never seen the entire city laid out so neatly before. The mighty Seren River divided Tarah neatly into its east and west sides, with the massive white stone bridge, the Serenarch, the only way across. The other nine towers, one dedicated to each of the gods, and one standing on a small isle amid the river for them all.

The entire city was alight with every color imaginable. Lanterns hung from every street corner, burning with enchanted flames. Some were charmed to burn a single different color all night long, others changed color by the minute. A different sort of light lit the sky. Magical lights danced across the night sky as bright as can be. These lights were conjured by Druadan all across the city, combining their powers to create a panorama that flashed and wound their way across the city. They were so bright that even the light of the stars seemed muted.

Except for the Ninestars, of course. The Ninestars gleamed a bright bluish light as they always did, hanging in their ever-present arc across the night sky. Even on cloudy nights when no other light could be seen in the darkness. The Ninestars were always there.

Sounds rose from all over the city as well. Music welled up from every part of Tarah. They did not play the same songs or even similar rhythms, but they seemed to come together in a magical harmony just the same.

Elodan basked in the wonder of what he was seeing. He had seen festivals before from the window of his bedroom. He had listened to the beautiful cacophony of singing voices as he fell asleep. But this was different. Seeing and hearing it all from above was like being one of the gods themselves. Looking down on the beauty and majesty of the Shining Silver City, the Gem of Serendin, the River Vale, was breathtaking.

Of course, because Talorin was their teacher, he soon turned the focus of his starry-eyed students to matters of scholarship. He began by quizzing them on the history of the Festival of Spring Dawning. Between the three of them, they managed to give satisfactory answers, though he could tell he did not have their full attention. After some time, Talorin was almost willing to give in to his pupils' desire to simply enjoy the festival. But he had one more bit of history to cover first.

"Dorilla, could you please tell us all the history of the shaping of the world? And how we came to be here now?" Talorin asked the young girl. She nodded hesitantly before launching into her answer.

"The Nine Gods created the world from the void between the stars. They created the earth for us to walk, the sea for us to sail, and the sky to watch over us. They created the beasts of the earth, the fish of the sea, and the birds of the air." Dorilla explained confidently. "Lastly, they created the Faen and the mortals. The Faen was tasked with guarding the creations of the gods while they slept, tired from their many labors. The race of Men was tasked with giving order and justice to the world where they ruled. Centuries back, after a great war, an alliance between men and Faen bore unexpected fruit. And that fruit was us, the Druadan. Our race came from the mingling of Faen and mortals. And as the Faen became less populous and retreated from the world, we took their place as protectors of the natural world." She finished her tale and looked at Talorin.

"Very good, Dorilla," Talorin said with a smile. "Jarin, could you please name each of the gods for us? And explain their domains?" Jarin nodded solemnly. This was not a particularly hard question, but woe to the student who got even part of it wrong. The gods were an essential part of the Druadan culture.

"Vinaya, of course, is the Lady of the Sky, who kindled all the stars into being," Jarin began. "Pteros is the Lord of all things that fly, for He gave them life. Hares is the Lord of Storms; He controls all the winds and his wrath is in every storm." He paused to clear his throat before continuing. "Gaela is the Mother of the earth. She created all the lands and made them fertile. Celebdos is the Lord of all the things that grow from the earth. He gave life to all the trees and plants of the world. And Orios is the Lord of beasts. He gave life to all the things that live on the land." Another pause to clear his throat. "Neros is the Father of the seas. He created the wide oceans and holds their might in His hands. Ketam is the Lady of the beasts of the sea. All things that live under the water are Hers. Naia is the Lady of the rivers. She created the freshwaters that we might find sustenance in them."

"Well said, Jarin," Talorin said, smiling again. He was about to pose his question to Elodan when a scream rent the night air. Their attention had been turned toward the north side of the city; the cry came from the south. They turned to the south and were stunned by what they saw.

A large mass of figures was gathered beyond the southern gates of the city. A large number had already poured through into the city proper. It was difficult to make out much of this strange group other than that they bore torches and numbered in at least the thousands. The Druadan, never a particularly numerous people, only numbered around two thousand in the city in total.

More screams began to pierce the night air. Gaps appeared in the display of magical lights overhead. A group of Druadan could be seen meeting with the front line of the strange company, a short-lived meeting it proved to be. The strangers fell on the small group and although it was hard to see details, it was apparent they were attacking them.

More of the attackers poured through the gates, moving up the city'. The light show had stopped now, and the city's inhabitants had begun to defend themselves. Elodan had never seen a Druad use magic for combat before, but even from this lofty perch, he could tell it was happening now. Explosions of stone broke out in spots where Druadan called upon the earth to stop the attackers. Bursts of flame sprouted in the night, and along the river, large spouts of water flew into the air and crashed down upon the crowds of invaders.

But as evident as it was that the magic being wielded below was significant, it was also clear that it was unlikely to prove enough. There were simply too many attackers.

"Who are they!?!?" Elodan screamed.

"It does not matter," the teacher responded. "We must go. Now!" He grabbed Dorilla by the arm and pushed her towards the door back into the tower. He ushered Jarin and Elodan after her. "They are on this side of the river. We must get to the Serenarch. Perhaps we can hold the east side against them." They hurried down the massive stairs as quickly as they dared, reaching the entry hall in a fraction of the time it had taken them to ascend earlier.

They burst onto the street outside the Tower, seeing groups of Druadan rushing south toward the Serenarch, hoping to make it there before the violent invaders could take it. The sounds were worse down here. Elodan could hear screaming all around him. Explosions rang out across the city. But there was no time for dwelling on it yet.

Talorin guided them toward the main southward street, joining them with a larger group of fleeing Druadan. Several times on their flight, Elodan caught sight of the attackers through alleyways or across open squares. They were easier to make out now, with their torches and the occasional raging fire to illuminate them. They wore grey robes belted with hempen rope and carried crude weapons; nothing more sophisticated than cudgels and rods of iron.

They paused for a moment at an intersection to catch their breaths, and Elodan took the opportunity to relate his observations to Talorin.

"I noticed," Talorin replied, wheezing slightly. "They are followers of the false god Sha. They have always hated our kind, but I never believed they would take such open violent action as this. The king in Coronar will not abide their fanaticism after this." There was no more time for talk as they were forced to move again; a group of the fanatics had spotted them and begun to pursue them. Three of the Druadan turned to face them instead of fleeing.

Elodan paused, wanting to yell at them to run, but Talorin gripped his shoulder tightly and pulled him along.

"They have made their choice, Elodan. We must honor them by ensuring their sacrifice is not in vain." And with that, they were on the run again. They reached the River Road and continued following it south toward the bridge. It was not much farther now.

A sudden explosion burst from the mouth of an alley on their right. Elodan saw two bodies fly through the air and crash onto the paving stones of the road. He looked to his left and saw a black-robed figure standing in the alley. It had its black cowl pulled low over its face and one arm extended toward them; a pale hand and wrist, as white as milk, uncovered by the sleeve of its robe.

"*Ninthe!*" Talorin gasped, looking pale. Before anyone else could move, the old man leapt in front of the group, thrusting his staff toward the alley and calling out in the Old Tongue, the language of magic. The two buildings on either side of the alley exploded. Stone and dust rained down as the building collapsed into the gap between them. Elodan could not tell if they came down on the black-robed figure or if they blocked the way, but it did not matter.

"Run!" Talorin screamed at the rest of the group, and run they did. Elodan looked back, fearing that he would see his teacher making a stand like the three Druadan who had stayed behind earlier and was relieved to see Talorin staggering along at the back of the group. Whatever he had done to collapse those buildings had taken a lot out of him.

Elodan could see Dorilla and Jarin at the head of the group, sprinting faster now as the base of the Serenarch came into view. It only took a few more moments before they had all reached the bridge and began to cross it.

They were all out of breath as they reached the apex of the mighty span. They paused looking around. Elodan gasped for air, struggling to stay upright. Until a massive grinding, splintering sound erupted from the south.

It was the sound of a Tower falling.

Elodan watched in horror as the massive spire dedicated to Orios toppled like a tree whose base had been wrenched from the ground. It was utterly unbelievable. This city, particularly the Towers, had been crafted by full-blooded Faen at the height of their craft. Made in ways that the Druadan no longer understood, these Towers should have been able to survive anything. Yet one had fallen. A sinking feeling in his gut told Elodan that it would not be the only one to fall this night.

"What was that thing?" Elodan asked Talorin as the rest of the group stood staring at where Orios' Tower had once been.

"It was one of the *Ninthe,* the Fallen," Talorin answered reluctantly. "Or, so I believe anyway. To think that one of them, or gods save us, more than one! That they might be here at the same time as this assault from the fanatical priests bodes very ill for us." A pained look flashed across his face. "We may need to abandon the city."

The group was almost ready to move on when a chorus of angry, shouting voices arose from the eastern base of the bridge. Torchlight heralded the approaching horde of fanatics as they streamed out of the streets and mounted the rise of the bridge. Talorin sighed a sound of resignation that Elodan had never thought he would hear from his teacher.

"You must all go now," He spoke to the group as a whole, but his eyes held Elodan's. "Do not stop until you reach the foothills of the mountains to the west. Perhaps they will be satisfied with driving us from the city." He said it as if he did not believe it, and Elodan agreed that it seemed unlikely.

The crowd of invaders was getting close now, surging across the span of the Serenarch with speed born of pure hate. At their head was an old man with a long white beard streaked with black. His dark eyes gleamed with a fevered rage in the light of the torch he carried. Talorin turned and faced the oncoming marauders, standing tall with his staff held in front like it might save him from the same dire fate that so many of their people had already met that night.

That was the last sight Elodan had of Talorin before he turned and fled with the rest of the soon to be refugees.

They fled through the streets, heading for the west gate of the city. They moved as quickly as they could, gathering other survivors as they went. They soon streamed through the gate, but still did not slow.

After hours of flight, they found themselves huddled atop one of the higher foothills of the western Vale. Elodan was relieved to discover that his mother was among the refugees, but grieved beyond thought when she told him that his father had stayed behind to fight. He stood with the others, staring down at the rape of the Shing Silver City. They watched as the final Tower fell, shattering into pieces mid-air and crashing into the mighty Seren. The city was full of fires, burning red throughout the different sections of the city. But most horrific was the otherworldly, shadowy black flame that engulfed the Serenarch. It burned and burned until the mighty span shattered in the center and plunged into the river.

Elodan stood in that spot for hours. He stood there through the night and into the dawn. He stood there even as everyone else began to gather up whatever they might have thought to bring with them. He stood there as the others discussed where they might go now.

Elodan stood there, watching the end of the Ten Towers of Tarah.

The Coming Storm

The last light of the setting sun was at the back of the two men who stood upon the western edge of the valley. They stood in silence, contemplating the scene before them. This valley had once been a lush, verdant place home to hundreds of generations over thousands of years. It was no longer so.

The valley was bare and dry now. The only vegetation was the blackened remnants of trees; twisted and dead, fruitless branches extended toward the darkening sky like the clawing fingers of a withered hand. The soil was no longer dark and fertile; it was dusty and sere. A few half-buried ruins were all that remained to indicate this land had once been inhabited.

Fel Narnir took in the ruined land stoically, his lank brown hair falling in a curtain around his tanned face. The man beside him, Rath Dinan, was equally impassive, his dark eyes were cold onyx chips set in his narrow, scarred face, and his long black hair was pulled back into a tail that hung down his back. Both men wore swords on their hips, with large shields slung across their backs. They had been expecting this since the first stories of the monster they were hunting first reached their ears. There was no sign of the beast yet, but it was only a matter of time.

"Is it here, do you think?" Fel broke the silence; his voice sounded glaringly out of place in this mortal world, though he had spoken softly. Rath scanned the surrounding hills to the south, all the way around the valley to the towering peak of Orys Tal in the north. Orys Tal was an enormous mountain that dominated the valley, its craggy summit a constant point against the sky.

"At the moment?" Rath responded dully, "Probably not. But I believe its lair must be near here."

Fel nodded. He knew they shared the same guess as to where the beast had made its abode. He could not imagine a better home for it than Orys Tal. It would take almost a full day to hike across the valley and reach the foot of the great mountain; neither of them made to start the journey.

Not yet. They had to be sure.

If they could stop it here, perhaps they could stop the rest of what was to come. He looked up into the sky, the Ninestars already visible in the oncoming twilight, burning in their ever-present arc across the sky. There was still hope.

Before Fel could say anything more to Rath, a sound like a distant thunderclap boomed to the north. They turned toward the mountain as the booming repeated itself, again and again. A wind rose throughout the valley as a shape rose from the northern horizon. It swooped toward Orys Tal, a creature of death on wings of shadow. The winged figure alit on the side of the mountain near the top and folded its great bat-like wings against its body, slithering into some massive yet unseen hole in the mountain.

Fel and Rath looked at each other, then started down the side of the valley. They did not need words to communicate that this was what they were searching for and that it was time to move. It took them a while to reach the valley floor, and it would be quite a walk to even reach Orys Tal, let alone scale it.

They walked for most of the night, stopping only a few hours before dawn to rest.

They could not risk lighting a fire, so they sat chilled and tired, chewing cold rations as the stars wheeled overhead.

"Do you know much of this place?" Fel asked, breaking the long silence. "I found little in my studies other than that they call this world Karres." Rath finished chewing the hard bread he was chewing and took a swig from his waterskin.

"I know a bit more than that," Rath said. "This place," he gestured to the valley around them, "has been known by many different names over the centuries. Harnan Vale, the Bowl of Blood, Victory Valley, and others besides. As to the larger world, I know this country was called Kendar at one point." He shrugged and took another drink. "It's not much, but this place has seen little of our kind during its existence. So, the records are scant."

"What about the beast?" Fel asked after a moment's pause. "Do you have any idea how we are supposed to slay a dragon?" Rath looked at him consideringly, then patted the sword that hung at his hip.

"*I* don't," Rath said, "but I've heard some stories."

"Your Shard fought a dragon!?!?" Fel asked. "But dragons are the spawn of Neth Gellin! How could anyone from Trallis have fought one?"

"My Shard did not fight one," Rath answered, calmly. "But they have legends of these beasts on Trallis. And my Shard remembers some of these tales." He stood and pulled his shield off of his back. He slid the leather covering off it, revealing a metal surface polished to a mirror shine. "The most common theme of these tales is that dragons have a mesmerizing stare. The best way to combat that is to reflect that gaze back at them and catch them in their own snare. Or so the stories say." He shrugged, slid the shield back over his shoulder and took his seat.

"So, we have no actual information on if your strategy will work or if this beast can even *be* killed?" Fel said, an air of almost desperation creeping into his voice.

"That about sums it up." Rath stood, tucking his waterskin into his belt. The sun was beginning to slip over the eastern horizon. "We should move on." With that, he turned and began to walk further into the valley.

Fel followed, shaking his head a bit. This was not going to be easy. They very well might die here on this withered shell of a world. But then again, Waylan was often sending them into trouble such as this. This was their purpose after all. To do the things no one else could. To keep the universe spinning as the gods had intended.

"Waylan told me a bit about you, you know," Fel said. Thinking about their mutual master had reminded him of some questions he wished to ask his companion.

"Oh? What did he say then?" He did not break stride nor even turn his head to facilitate the conversation. Most people would take that as a sort of dismissal, but Fel was not so easily dissuaded from a course.

"Well, he said you had pursued a long life of vengeance before entering his service, and that you were among the most capable and deadly beings alive in the universe today." Fel pretended to think, as if this last point were of no consequence. "He also said you may be entirely mad."

Rath grunted in response but voiced no objections or clarifications.

"Did he mention anything about me to you?" Fel prodded. He was unsure why he was so interested in what Waylan might have said about him, but he could not let it go. Rath turned on the spot and looked him hard in the eye.

"More or less the same things," Rath said it as simply as he said everything else. As if no word that passed his lips were of any consequence. But just before he turned back to continue walking, Fel thought he glimpsed a slight light in those dark eyes. As if Rath might have been making a joke.

They continued their hike for several more hours, the sun climbing in the sky until it hovered overhead. Despite the position and the exertion of their long walk, there was very little heat in the air. There was a perpetual haze in the air that seemed to not only dim the light of the sun but block its warmth as well. At the pace they were traveling, they would likely reach the mountain's base by nightfall.

"Have you ever met Isar?" Fel asked suddenly; the idea had been nagging at him for a while, but he finally felt he could hold it in no more. Rath glanced over his shoulder, his face as impassable as ever.

"Aye, I've met him," Rath answered.

"And did you speak to him? Did he tell you his plans?" Fel asked curiously.

"He did," Rath grunted. He did not slow his pace and only turned his head slightly to respond.

"What did you think of them?" Fel asked, well aware that he sounded like a pestering child at this point. It was just so hard to get any real talk out of his stoic partner.

"I think he is blind," Rath answered, sighing slightly. Fel wondered whether the sigh was for his numerous questions or at the absurdity of what Isar envisioned doing. "He is focused so hard on his goal that he cannot see how his meddling might lead to the very thing he most fears."

"And what is it he fears, do you think?" Fel pressed. He had his own theory, but he wanted to see if Rath had reached a similar conclusion before voicing his own.

"Simply put, he fears Asha'tamenar'ash being free. He fears the wrath that the Great Leech will visit upon the universe."

"I disagree," Fel said, not to provoke an argument, simply because he had to speak of his own thoughts before they drove him mad. "I think he wants Asha"tamenar'ash free."

"And why would he want that?" Rath asked, still not slowing his pace, but turning his head to look Fel in the face.

"Well," Fel began, "Waylan once told me that all the Faen lost friends and family to Asha'tamenar'ash's depredations before his foul designs were uncovered. It's likely that Isar did too. I believe he wants revenge. And so long as Asha'tamenar'ash remains fenced in Neth Gellin, Isar can never have his vengeance."

Rath was quiet for some time. He walked on, head down, as if in deep thought.

"There is some merit in that," Rath said, finally. "But if it is true, then he is taking an awful gamble that his plans will bring back the gods. Only with their help could his vengeance be achieved." He shook his head. "Perhaps not even with them."

Fel said no more on the subject. The fact that Rath had not dismissed his theory was reassuring. Although there was nothing either of them could do about it beyond what they were currently about.

They pressed on in silence, the sun descending toward the western horizon. The land began to rise as they neared the north end of the valley and the broad, sloping skirts of Orys Tal. They stopped for a brief rest at the mountain's base, dusk deepening around them.

"I can get us up to whatever cave the beast used in a few hours," Fel offered. He calculated how much of his animus it would take to shadow-jump them up the mountain. It would be a strain, but not beyond his abilities.

"You would be in no shape to fight if you did," Rath pointed out.

"True, but we could rest at the top and be ready to move as soon as possible," Fel answered. "Plus, climbing in the normal fashion will exhaust me as well. Not to mention it will take twice as long. At least." Rath pondered what Fel said, his chin on his hands. After some time, he spoke.

"Very well. Let me know when you are ready."

"Soon," Fel responded. "Just to be sure, you can use your abilities here, right? I never gave thought to how your Absorption might work in a world with no ley lines."

"I do not need ley lines except on Olthos," Rath answered. "On any of the other nine worlds, I can draw from the Spark itself. So long as the Spark is here, I will have full access to my powers."

"Good," Fel said. They would both need access to the fullness of their abilities to take down the monster that resided in the mountain.

After an hour of rest, Fel indicated to Rath that he was ready. He took Rath by the elbow and, drawing upon the Essence of Stealth, stepped into the nearest shadow. They emerged from a different shadow several hundred feet up from where they had been. Fel repeated this process until they found themselves standing outside a massive hole in the side of the mountain. If the hole size was any indication, the beast they were after was even bigger than they had thought.

Fel collapsed in exhaustion beside the mouth of the yawning tunnel. Rath set about making a small camp. He pulled a bedroll from his pack and laid it out before gently pushing Fel onto it.

"Sleep, if you can," Rath said sternly. "I'll keep watch. You need to recover." Fel wanted to argue that he was no child in need of mothering, but his eyes were heavy, and he gave in to sleep easier than he would have liked to admit.

Fel awoke to the full dark of midnight. Rath had kindled a tiny fire of dried sticks nearby. The fire gave no smoke and hardly any light, but it was better than nothing, especially with the strange, noxious haze being even stronger now.

Fel took stock of his condition. He was rested and his animus felt as full as he could hope for it to be.

"When should we go in?" Fel asked. "I am ready when you are and frankly, eager to get his done with." Rath opened his mouth to speak when another voice cut him off.

"We should hurry if you intend to stop the beast," the voice said. "It will leave again in the morning if its habits are anything to go by." Fel reached for his sword at the same time as Rath. They stood in unison, facing the shadows from which the voice had come.

A figure stepped into the dim light of the fire. It was tall and thin, dressed in blood-red robes, with a heavy cowl pulled low over its face. Its hands were folded into the sleeves of its robes and from its belt hung an assortment of pouches and tubes.

"No need to fear," the thing said. "I came to answer the same summons as you." It pulled back its hood, revealing the pale, thin face of a man. The man was bald and his face was clean-shaven. His cheeks were hollow and his brown eyes were large in his face. In pulling his hood back, his sleeves had fallen to reveal two pale, thin forearms adorned with silvery scars.

"Who or what are you?" Rath said, his voice calm, but his body as tight as a bowstring, ready to snap.

"I am called Malketh," the man said. "As to what I am, I am a Runewarden." The man folded his hands back inside the sleeves of his robes. "And if I may anticipate your next question, I am here because Waylan sent me." He eyed Fel and Rath with an appraising air. "He thought you might find my abilities useful."

"If Waylan sent you, then you must know the cipher," Rath responded. "What lies at the heart of the shadow?" Rath stared at Malketh, hand still tight on the hilt of his sword.

"The never-sated hunger," Malketh responded with no hesitation. Rath relaxed immediately. Fel wanted to relax; the strange man had answered correctly, but it was hard to let his guard down.

"What exactly are the abilities of a Runewarden?" Rath asked. "I confess I did not know that there were any of you left."

"We have many different talents," Malketh answered. "But my specialties lie in blood and bondage." He shifted slightly as if uncomfortable. "As to the rarity of my kind. There are very few of us are left. I am the only one who saw the wisdom of Waylan's path. The rest have gone from this world, though I know not where."

"And how might your talents serve us," Fel asked. "We have a strategy in mind already." This was not exactly true. They had not discussed the details of the plan, though Fel was confident in his part. And it was true that the larger part hinged on a centuries-old myth that Rath had gleaned from his Shard. Still, he had a hard time trusting this stranger.

"I'm afraid I will be of little use," Malketh began, "unless you can draw blood from the monster. But if you do, I can bind it and hold it. For a time at least. Long enough for you to strike a mortal blow if indeed, such a thing is possible." Fel wanted to point out the unlikelihood that they would draw blood unless the monster were fully subdued, in which case they would not need Malketh's help. But Rath spoke first.

"Then the plan is simple," Rath said. "Fel will use his Essences to slow or hold the beast. I will use my mirror shield to force its paralytic gaze back on itself. Then I will strike a blow. If I fail to kill it, then Malketh can use its blood to bind it until we can finish the job." Fel thought it sounded too simple when Rath laid it out like that. However, he could find no alternative that held realistic answers. Malketh nodded in agreement to the plan.

Rath quickly broke down the hastily assembled camp, and soon the trio was ready to head into the mountain. Upon entering the massive tunnel, they noticed how sharply it sloped downward. They followed it carefully, sometimes having to shuffle their steps to avoid sliding down the steep incline.

In time, the tunnel leveled out. It narrowed a bit before opening into an enormous hollow cavern. The ceiling was at least a hundred yards above their heads. The bottom…

The bottom was thousands of feet down.

The cavern's walls fell in sheer sides straight down to the bottom of what must have been the very center of the mountain. All was dark except for the very bottom, where a bright orange-red glow lit a large circle in the floor. Worst of all, there was no possible way to get to the bottom of the lair.

Except one.

"I guess I'll have to shadow jump us down there," Fel said. He tried to say it casually, but he felt the slight quaver in his voice. Shadow-jumping three people that far would be difficult, even though traveling down was much easier than traveling up.

"Are you sure?" Rath asked, eyeing him warily.

"I am," Fel answered. "Not that we're spoiled for choice."

Fel motioned for the other two to come closer, then took them each by the elbow. He guided them toward the nearest shadow, drew upon his animus, and stepped into the nothingness. They emerged, stumbling, onto a rocky outcrop of land just outside the fiery ring of what could now be clearly seen as lava.

Inside the circle of sluggish fire was the beast. It was more than two hundred feet long and thick in the body. Its massive wings were tucked snugly to its sides. It had four legs, each with four razor-tipped claws on each foot. It was curled in sleep, its head tucked into its side, long tail curled around itself like some hellish, black-scaled cat. The black scales that made up its entire body were strange to behold. They seemed to drink in the light of the fiery circle. They looked almost insubstantial, although Fel guessed each scale was as hard as a diamond and tougher than pig iron.

Fel looked at his companions and could tell they were just as fazed as he was. This was a monumental task, and part of him doubted if they were up to it.

"Let's go," Rath whispered. "Just as we discussed." He took a running start and leapt over the ring of lava. He landed almost silently on the other side and began to move toward the beast's head. The Runewarden moved into the shadows at the edge of the lava and settled himself in a crouch to wait his turn.

Fel stepped back into the shadows and tapped his animus, shadow-jumping through the darkness. He reappeared a dozen yards above the dragon's back, falling with no hesitation onto its back just where the neck met the body. He felt the beast shift suddenly as it felt his presence. He immediately tapped into the Essence of Spirit and slammed both hands onto the beast's back. He sent Spirit energy into the monster, searching for its animus. It was hard to find, and for a moment, he worried that this strange creature might not have one.

But all living things have an animus, and Fel found the dragon's at last. He was dimly aware of Rath shouting and pulling his Soulshard from the sheath at his hip. He had a dim awareness through the dragon's eyes of a small man holding a sword that glowed from a triangle of strange metal near the hilt.

Fel focused harder on freezing the dragon's animus, but it was a mighty task. The creature's animus was like no other he had felt. It was not a shining reservoir of power; instead, it was a writhing black mass that fought and evaded his attempts to subdue it. He managed to latch onto part of it, but that proved of little use. The monster roared and reared, nearly unseating Fel. He could tell that only Rath's enhanced speed and reflexes had saved him so far.

Fel was seeing double now. Partly through the dragon's eyes and partly through his own. Rath had pulled his mirror shield and was trying to catch the monster's gaze on its reflective service. The beast was too quick and canny for it.

The dragon darted its head at Rath again and again.

Rath evaded it again and again.

Fel continued to pour Spirit Essence from his animus into the dragon's, desperately trying to bring it under his will. But it was futile. The creature was too foreign and too powerful.

Rath seemed to have given up on using the shield and was now attempting to hack at the massive, darting head of the monster. It seemed he might land a blow until he stumbled inexplicably. He fell to one knee as the edge of the dragon's jaw his leg. He was vulnerable now, trapped on one leg, as the dragon reared back for a final strike.

Fel changed his tactics. Instead of pouring Spirit into the dragon, he threw up a wall of shadow before the beast's eyes. Its striking jaws missed Rath by a mere foot, leaving its eye level with the injured man.

Rath raised his Shard and plunged it into the dragon's eye. The monster pulled back just in time to avoid a mortal blow. But it was enough to stain the blade with the beast's blood.

Rath rolled to the side and threw his blade, end over end, to stick into the rocky floor near Malketh.

Malketh rushed forward, pulling a silver dagger from his belt. He pulled the blade across his forearm, opening a gash that pulsed blood into his palm. The Runewarden brushed his other hand down the blade of Rath's Soulshard and then began to draw in the air. He drew an odd symbol in the air with each hand, the blood leaving his hand and becoming solid in the air. The figure he drew became solid and burned like fire, hanging in the air before Malketh.

"Hurry!" Malketh screamed, falling to his knees. "Kill it!"

"Rath!" Fel shouted, drawing his own Shard. "Take it!" He tossed the sword down to Rath, who caught it deftly. Rath stumbled to his feet and hobbled toward the dragon. The monster was stuck, its head quivering just a foot off the ground. Rath pulled the sword back and plunged into the blood red iris of the dragon's eye. The blade sank into the soft tissue all the way to the hilt.

Black blood fountained from the wound. The creature began to convulse, and Fel could feel through its tainted animus that it was in its death throes. He shadow-jumped from the creature's back and appeared next to Malketh, who had sunken to his knees and was in apparent agony.

The symbols that Malketh had drawn in the air faded and vanished as the beast's struggle slowed, then stopped altogether. Fel gave the Runewarden his arm, and the two limped toward where Rath was just leaping back over the rim of the circle of lava.

"Do you think you can jump us back to the top?" Rath asked, sweat flowing freely from his forehead.

Fel nodded, holding tight to Malketh and grabbing Rath's arm. He lurched toward the nearest shadow and drew upon his animus once more.

The trio appeared out of the darkness near the mouth of the tunnel. They clung to each other, hobbling back up the steep slope to the opening in the side of the mountain. They reached the opening and collapsed in a heap.

"What happened, Rath?" Fel asked after gasping to regain his breath. "It was like you ran out of energy all at once." Rath shook his head, a look of misery on his face.

"The Spark is gone," Rath said. "I do not know if it has been taken from this world or destroyed. But it is gone." Fel blanched at the news. One of the tragedies they had been sent to avert, perhaps the larger part of their goal, had come to pass.

It was almost dawn as the three men sat panting on the side of Orys Tal.

"Look!" Malketh said breathlessly.

They all looked up to see nine bluish-white stars, more prominent than usual, shoot across the sky and vanish from view.

The Ninestars had fallen.

A distant noise dragged their attention from the starless sky. Off to the east, the sun was beginning to rise. Against the pale yellow of the rising sun, several dark shapes wheeled and flapped through the air.

First, it was a couple. Then several. Then a dozen. Then countless more.

"What is this?" Fel asked in disbelief.
Rath's voice was despairing as he responded.

"It's the beginning of the end."

Made in United States
North Haven, CT
01 May 2023